When Ethan's wagon rolls to a stop Mary kneels down on the ground in front of my outstretched paws and places her two hands on my head.

"Tobias, Tobias," she says, "don't ever let other people tell you who you are. Their mirrors are so cloudy and distorted, the images all twisted by their own fears and misunderstandings. Your one true reflection is in the eye of your Creator. Oh, Tobias, in the beginning God saw all that was and all that would ever come into being. That's when your own Creator said, 'It is very good.'" Her fingers are tickling the fur behind both of my ears, and everything fits together, her words and the dance of creation and the feel of her hands on my head. It is all very good, and I am once again balanced in my proper place.

Then a shrill little voice calls out, "You, Girl, let me see that dog!"

MARY'S DOG

Glenn Lamb McCoy

To Linda—
with love—

COPYRIGHTS AND DISCLAIMER

This is a work of fiction. The angel Gabriel, Mary, her parents, Joseph, Elizabeth, Zechariah, and King Herod are Biblical figures. All other characters in this book are products of the author's imagination and any resemblance to people living or dead is purely coincidental. The dog, however, may be quite real. Who knows?

ISBN: 978-1-63492-665-2

DEDICATION

For my husband Richard,

my constant lifeline to the heart of God.

Contents

A NOTE ABOUT NAMES

Several of the characters in this novel are called by more than one name.

Don't blame the author, blame the dog.

Bellator/ Tobias

My Master/ Jeremiah

The driver/ Ethan

The Lady/ Rebekah

The young man/ Abraham

Levanah/ Esther

The child/ Sara

The caravan leader/ Josiah

ACKNOWLEDGMENTS

I begin with deep gratitude for my mother, Josephine Gleason Lamb, who walked through this world seeing the people around her through eyes of compassion. The older I get, the more I appreciate her quiet yet feisty example. My vision of Mary is rooted in my mother's soul.

Many thanks to my big sisters, Ann-Marie, Joie, Helen, and Gusti- the Five Lamb Girls, a.k.a. "The Battling Lambs." We sharpened each other's wits, learned to forgive, cried on each other's shoulders, and still managed to keep laughing all the way. (Helen, we miss you every day.) I thank them for all the second chances enjoyed by the characters in this book.

Thanks as well to the faith family of St. Stephen Church in Winter Springs, Fl, led by the one and only Rev. John Bluett, for an atmosphere of welcome and generosity toward all. During my years leading Adult Education along with worship and prayer groups, I have received much more than you can imagine. Listening with love to all the stories you shared with one another over the years has helped my Mary enter into the lives of the people she meets on her journey.

For my first readers: my weekly faith-sharing group, Evelyn Hinson, Kathy Salmieri, and Cheryl McGowen, for their ideas and encouragement (sometimes including necessary badgering); for Flora Torra and Betty Lacey, whose deep and understanding hearts add so much to my writing and my own approach to the world; for Ellie Stefanik, who kept pushing me just hard enough; for Martawn Reese and her unique perspective; for Janelle McCoy's young mother's view and Kaitlyn McCoy's take as a college student; and for the Buena H. S. Divas, who tirelessly cheer each other on in all our very diverse endeavors: gratitude and blessings to each one of you. Heartfelt thanks to Caryl DeGrandi for her friendship, bad puns, and stellar editorial guidance, and to Ann-Marie for a key suggestion. All these and others who have taken the time to read and comment on this book have carried me along on a wave of grace, and I am very thankful.

There's a special place in my heart for those who brought to birth the original cover art. For Gusti, who dragged me from Florida to New Hampshire for two weeks in January for the block print art class at Plymouth University with professor emerita Annette Mitchell, and for the wonderful and gifted artists who showered me with creativity and acceptance. You unlocked something I didn't know I had, and I will never forget you. Undying thanks to Annette for continuing care above and beyond what anyone could reasonably expect as I struggled through the evolution of my cover design. I am grateful for artistic input from Gusti as well as from Kathy, Cheryl, Evelyn, Betty, Flora, and Janelle. Much appreciation to Zoran Milovokovic of Shara Kennel for the photos of his modern-day descendants of the Molossi breed. Special thanks to professional photographer Linda Womack Ekstrum for so freely offering her time and expertise (and her "eye", as well as her discerning "no".)

Thanks to our children Greg and Rich, our daughters-in-law Kristi and Janelle, and our grandchildren, Kaitlyn, James. Will and Haley, for keeping me grounded. Our sons say we've given them roots and wings, but they give these two necessary gifts back to me every day. Each one of you has helped me to keep Mary real.

There are no words sufficient to thank my husband Richard. Abbot Thomas Keating once told us the purpose of marriage is to process one another's shadow. Writers are often creatures of contrast with lots of shadows that may take some heavy lifting in the processing department. God has blessed me with a soulmate who is up to the job. All I can offer him in return is what my wise scientist-musician father James promised Dick before our wedding: that I would make his life "interesting."

And finally, my thanks to all the dogs who have shared my home and my life over the years. The Book of Job was right: the animals have much to teach us about the presence of God in our world. Dogs have shown me so many living examples of unconditional love, patient suffering, faithfulness, the importance of play, and the sheer joy of living in the moment. (Our cats have also been instructive, but that's a topic for another day.)

THE SOUL OF EVERY LIVING THING

You have only to ask the animals,
for them to instruct you,
and the birds in the sky,
for them to inform you.
The creeping things of earth
will give you lessons,
and the fish of the sea
provide you an explanation:
there is not one such creature but will know
that the hand of God has arranged things like this!
In God's hand is the soul of every living thing
and the breath of every human being!

Job 12: 7-10[i]

PREFACE

This is a work of fiction, a product of both my imagination and years of wondering. What was Mary of Nazareth like? There is no clear and complete answer in the Bible or in any historical records. All attempts to create an image of her with paint, marble, melody or words are necessarily creative efforts, not fact-based representations.

Since love demands expression and Mary is deeply loved by many, we persist. Throughout the centuries we have met this young mother-to-be from 1st century Israel as a blue-eyed blonde, an Italian peasant, a well-dressed medieval noblewoman, a stiff and stern-faced matron, and countless other variations. She has been a member of every race on earth. She has been slender, voluptuous, sturdy, and child-like. All of these versions of her coexist in a rich panorama, happily standing side-by-side like members of a huge family posing for a picture at a reunion picnic.

This time Mary comes to the picnic in the company of a dog. Remember: this is fiction. The dog in this story is a constant reminder that imagination is at work here. This is not Biblical exegesis, although the narrative is woven from threads firmly attached to the scriptures and the historical record. The Gospel of Luke, the Book of Psalms, Roman military records, ancient caravan life, the memory of the lost Molossus breed of war-dogs: all this and more has been carefully researched.

The particular fictional dog himself is another matter. He appeared by my side as I was contemplating that small span of days between the angel Gabriel's visit to Mary and her arrival at Elizabeth's home. Like most dogs, he wanted to come along for the ride. How could I refuse?

DAY ONE

You have only to ask the animals,

for them to instruct you..."

Job 12: 7[ii]

Chapter 1 -

I love the first light of morning and I love walks, so today is already very good. Fresh dew tickles my paws with each step, and my nose quivers with unfamiliar scents, tantalizing hints and promises of what awaits on the road ahead. I inhale deeply, paying no heed to the shouts and whispers that surround me. "Look at the size of that monster." "Watch out." "Filthy animal." "Ama, I'm scared." These words are not new to me, and I do not find them interesting.

Before we go any farther I should explain something. People guess that since dogs do not talk in human words, we do not understand human words. This guess is wrong. Whatever we hear, we take in. Not all the words make sense to us, but we remember them. Our memories are clear, and they are long. We do not ponder what is past, or chew over it like old bones. For us, what is done is done. But we remember. Sometimes a person who takes the time to look into our eyes will say to one of us, "You understand, don't you, boy?" When we hear this we wag our tails, but we do not take it very seriously.

I myself am a Molossus, the most important breed in the Roman empire. We keep watch. We pay attention. It is our nature and our job. Because of this I notice her at once, in spite of the sights and smells of the merchant's camp that churn around us: sweating men, the swirling smoke of cook-fires, tethered camels dropping fresh dung as they sway from foot to foot, the cloth of musty tents flapping in the morning sun, and detestable donkeys throwing back their heads and braying their foul breath into the air. She stands in the center of all this, one small island of stillness and silence. Even the veil that covers her head and shoulders is motionless, although I can feel a breeze tickling my whiskers.

The wind is blowing in my direction and I detect the metallic scent of anxiety, but it is not coming from her. I sniff the air and trace the source to the tall man standing at her side. His eyes shift from face to face as he searches the crowd. When my Master starts to move toward the tall man and the girl I follow without needing a tug on my leash. My tail sweeps from side to side as I walk. Every part of me is already eager to be near her, even though I know my chances of getting close are poor. Except for the Roman troops, nearly everyone in this country calls dogs 'unclean.' My Master once questioned his friend the rabbi about this, and after the man had unrolled many scrolls and muttered and grumbled for a whole afternoon he could find nothing in the writings or teachings stating that it is so. Still, most people shrink back when they see one of us coming.

Just steps away now, I can see the shaking of the tall man's hand as he clutches the rope around a lumpy bundle of cloth. He holds on to it the way fresh recruits at the Roman camp where my Master works clench the sword-hilts before their first battle-practice, with sweat dripping from their palms. We war-dogs find them amusing.

At last we reach them, and the girl moves. Her hand reaches toward me and brushes across the fur behind my left ear- my favorite spot. With this one unexpected touch I belong to her.

Being a girl in the company of men she does not speak. The tall man says, "Greetings, son of my old friend, and may the Lord bless you." He hands my Master the cloth bundle and also a small pouch that jingles faintly. He continues, "This is the price we agreed on for my daughter's passage. Promise again that you'll escort her in safety and see her all the way to the door of her kinsman's house." His words tremble like his hands. "Her mother and I are placing our trust in you."

My Master nods and answers with a long and solemn speech full of the reassuring sounds he makes when he's handling new pups. All the while he weighs the pouch in his hand.

The tall man turns to face the girl and puts his hands on her shoulders. He says, "Mary, child of my heart, it's not too late to change your mind. I have to ask you one more time: are you sure about this journey?"

Mary. Her name is Mary. She says, "Yes, Father. This is my pathway." Her voice is low, and my ears twitch with pleasure at the sound of it.

She continues, "Oh, Abba, I know this must be hard for you. You always tell us, 'Don't rush, take your time,' but right now everything is happening so quickly. All of a sudden here we are, and the caravan's ready to leave. I already have Mother's blessing, so all I lack is yours. Please, Father. It's the only way we can all be at peace with this parting."

The man sighs. Moving as if his arms are weighted down with iron shackles, he lifts his hands and places them on the sides of Mary's head. His fingertips touch her just behind where her ears must be, there under the veil and her covered-up hair. Perhaps this is her favorite spot, too. Then he lifts his eyes to the sky as he recites words in a respectful tone, like the voice a centurion would use only when speaking to his commanding prefect. During this Mary stands with head bowed, her veil flowing down like warm water in the comfort of a steaming bathhouse. There may be great tension in the man, but Mary is at ease, there within her stillness.

The man's voice trails off and he bends down to kiss her forehead. It is a long kiss. Then he turns abruptly and walks away into the crowd. Mary raises a hand in farewell, but the man does not look back.

As she lowers her hand I push my nose under her palm to comfort her, and she responds by offering another scratch behind my ear. Too soon, my Master throws the rope of her bundle over his shoulder and says, "Right this way, Girl. I have a surprise for you."

We cut across the camp with Mary's hand resting lightly on my shoulder. She walks with her back straight and her spine properly stretched, so her hand is a comfortable match for my height. If she were a Roman recruit she would not need lessons in correct posture.

As we go my Master talks quickly, his eyes darting across the sky, the crowd, the treetops of a nearby olive grove-anywhere but the girl's face. "I promised to get you there in safety, so I've made arrangements for you to ride in a nice wagon with a fine lady who'll watch over you on the journey. She may ask you to do a few chores for her as you go along, but I'm sure you won't mind at all. After all, you'll be saving yourself all that walking and noise and…"

We have arrived at a hulking wooden wagon covered with a roof of dark matted felt stretched tightly over a frame of hoops. The cloth is steaming slightly as the sun burns off the morning dew. It smells of sheep, which is not as offensive to the nose as the odor of the donkeys harnessed at the front.

My Master drops the end of my leash to the ground and motions for me to sit. Next he tosses the bundle up onto the driver's seat and turns to offer Mary his hand. She bends down to look into my eyes as she scratches behind my ear one more time. Then she rises, places one foot firmly on the hub of the wooden wheel, swings herself up to the seat, and is swallowed by the great mouth of the covered wagon. I cannot keep myself from whining, which draws a sharp 'hsst' from my Master. He is correct. Roman war-dogs do not whine.

Next he too climbs into the wagon. I stand on my hind legs and leap toward the opening like an untrained whelp. Inside, my Master starts to speak. I do not defy him by actually pulling myself up and climbing into the wagon, but with my front paws resting against the side I can just make out the words.

Chapter 2

My Master is speaking as he does to the centurion. I cannot see him through the thick felt, but I know he is bowing, holding his hands folded in front of him, and making himself small. "Just as I promised", he is saying. "Such a great lady as yourself will appreciate her pleasant manner as well as her strong arms and back. She'll serve you well, all the way to your son's home. I assure you she will eat very little and come when she's bidden, by day and by night."

A new voice with the yappy tone of a lap-dog snaps out a command: "Come here, Girl, out of the shadows." There is a long pause. Then the voice says, "A bit young, but I suppose she will have to do. Payment to you at our destination, my man, but only if she proves satisfactory. Now go! You take up too much space."

Back on all fours, I wait at attention for Mary to come out of the wagon. However, only my Master emerges, shaking his head and muttering. Another whine escapes me, but my Master does not seem to notice. Instead he grabs my leash and lumbers off toward our campsite. When I hesitate he gives the leash a sharp jerk and I follow, head down, grieving the loss of Mary from my life.

The entire caravan is putting itself in order, nearly ready to depart. My Master grumbles, "What a mess. A simple one-day stop for the Shabbat, and people and belongings are scattered around like thrown dice. No discipline at all. Keeping track of this mob won't be easy, will it, Boy?"

We arrived yesterday after sundown and slept here last night, but unlike all the others my Master had our gear neatly packed this morning before dawn. Now my Master shoulders his pack and takes up his thick staff. His knife, as always, is tucked into the sheath on his belt. He is serving as one of the guards on this journey, so we report to the caravan leader's wagon, alert and ready to fight off whatever comes our way. As we begin our long walk through the countryside I relax into my job, ready for action.

Chapter 3

Even pace, head up, eyes scanning for movement, ears cocked for sounds that do not belong in a peaceful countryside, nose attuned to whatever comes to me on the breeze, my Master by my side: the caravan is safe, and I am content. I have known how to do this since I was still a puppy with my milk teeth, and do it very well. No harmless creatures scurrying nearby will scatter my attention, no matter how interesting or tasty they may be. No braying donkey or friendly shout will distract me. I have been trained very well to focus on danger instead of what is entertaining to most dogs, and I am proud of my ability to carry out what I have learned. Whenever my Master tells me to patrol, this is what I do. I hear him, and I obey.

When humans set out to train dogs, they think we do not obey because we do not understand. This is true of young pups, who pay no attention to human words at all, any more than they heed wind in the trees or the squawking of wild birds. To pups all is just noise except for the sounds their mother makes. Then they start to understand the yips of their littermates, and then the barking of other dogs. By the time we are grown, we can follow the words of the humans who surround us. So when we do not obey, it is hardly ever because we are unsure of what the master wants. Instead it is because we do not want to do it.

There are two methods people use to train dogs. One is want-not, and the other is want. In want-not, the human yells and beats and starves the dogs to force us to do something. If we want not to be yelled at or beaten or starved, we do what we are told. This is the way the Romans treat us. But if this kind of master turns his back on his dogs or leaves the gate open there is trouble, and sometimes death, for either dog or human.

The other is my Master's way. He treats me well and gives me the food I need, so that I want to do what he tells me. He also shows me the ways of Roman war-dogs, and then I want to be one of them. He lets the other dogs be my teachers. The Roman trainers used to mock my Master for his ways and call him stupid and weak, but now I am first among the war-dogs, and most of the other trainers do not speak to him at all.

All the mistakes humans make about dogs they also make about one another. The Romans do not know that the barbarian slaves serving in the encampment understand them. They think the slaves are truly inferior creatures, like donkeys. The Romans treat the slaves the same way they treat us dogs, with chains and collars and blows. But since I understand the speech of the barbarians as well as the Latin of the Romans and also the tongue of my Master and the other people of this land, I know that all of them think the same thoughts and say the same things among themselves. It is too cold. It is too hot. I am hungry. The sunlight feels good. I am bored. I am angry. I want a woman. I am telling a joke. Ha ha ha.

Why my Master still hesitates and struggles when he speaks Latin is a mystery to me. It does not seem that hard, but perhaps this is because I only need to listen and do not have to say words. People mostly talk about what they feel and what they do. If you can see what they are feeling and doing, then the patterns of the words they are using follow along, like rabbit tracks follow along after a rabbit. Learning the meanings of a new set of words is not difficult for us dogs. Any words that are not about feeling and doing do not matter, so we do not worry about them. In the end we understand what many of the other words mean, too, but they are not as important.

So this is what dogs do. While we are keeping watch, we listen and we mostly understand, even when we look like we are asleep.

Chapter 4

This first morning of our journey is clear and bright, ideal weather for our task of patrolling the whole length of the caravan. My Master slips off my leash and we begin. There is no hurry. There are many people traveling on foot, so the whole group moves no faster than a man or woman can walk. My Master says we will camp somewhere near a place called Scythopolis after a full day of travel, which he says would only be a pleasant morning's march for any self-respecting troop of Romans. This is an easy and enjoyable job, a stroll through a shallow valley with many fields full of enough growing grains to make my Master sneeze and mutter as we go along. I even get the chance to nip the flank of a pack donkey that refuses to move in the right direction because he has his nose buried in a wayside stand of wheat.

The donkey moves on, and as I am returning to my Master I feel the prickle of the hackles along my back rising up. A breeze carries a sharp scent laden with danger: there are wolves nearby. I turn my head in the direction of the threat and see a small boy squatting in the dirt just off the roadway as the caravan moves past him. He is the one who whimpered "Ama, I'm scared" when he saw me earlier. Now there is a real reason for fear, but he does not know the smell of wolf so he remains undisturbed. The child is humming as he stacks pebbles into the shape of a house, all of his attention fixed on his chore. Although he is very young there is no one taking care of him. Alone and unprotected, he is clearly the target of the unseen hunters now stalking him in the tall grass.

I launch myself on a straight line toward the wolves. As I pass the child I turn my head and snarl at him, the fastest way to send him running back to his Ama and to safety. He screams in terror as he races away, even though the risk is now over and no wolf will touch him.

I reach the predators' hiding place and find three males, two young ones with their older leader. The younger ones face off against me, making a show, growling and menacing, teeth bared to the gums. This means the leader is circling silently to attack my flank, a tactic as old as hunger. When I sense the moment of his leap behind me I spin and sink my teeth into the nape of his neck. In one motion I pivot, and with the whole weight of my body behind it I release my grip and catapult the leader into his companions. The three of them fall, tumbling in a tangle of limbs. The leader regains his feet in an instant and stands his ground, head lowered. Now there is respect in his eyes. He spits out a tuft of fur from my neck ruff, the only damage he was able to inflict.

Wolves are smart animals, smart enough to know there will be no easy prey for them on this caravan. Hunters hunt; I do not blame them for that. But these three are sleek and well-fed, not driven by thin ribs and desperation. Now they have been defeated by a larger and more skilled opponent. Besides, the child is gone, so continuing their attack would gain them nothing but more injuries. With a toss of his head the leader turns and limps away through the grass. The others fall in behind him in single file.

I return to the road and seek my Master, but now I am met with ripples of anger and fear coming at me from all sides. This does not make sense. I have conquered the wolves and rescued the boy, so these people should be greeting me as a hero. The child is still howling, but thanks to my bravery he is now safe in his Ama's arms. Sadly, since he did not see the wolves and I do not have a way to explain why I snarled at him, no one will ever tell the story of my victory.

When I find my Master he is surrounded by shouting people, so instead of approaching him I move back off the road into the grasses and patrol beside the caravan, hidden and confused. I did nothing wrong but still I feel guilt and shame, as if I have been caught stealing the Centurion's supper. I need my Master.

When it is time for the midday rest the caravan halts and people return to their own places. My Master comes to the side of the road and takes off his backpack. He finds a seat on the stump of an old tree and looks in my direction, which he could only do if he has been keeping track of my shadowing position here behind the tall grass. I move to his side with caution, unsure of my reception, but he seems unworried. "Well, Boy, you've had quite a morning. I've had twenty different stories yelled in my ear, and none of them make any sense. Did you growl at a little boy? Or did you drag him away from his mother and try to eat him like a barley-loaf?" My Master is smiling at me. He is not angry. "I wish you could talk, but it really doesn't matter. Whatever happened, Bellator, you're a good dog and I trust you."

All is well, and we are settling down for a well-earned break when a little man, thin like a stray cat, runs up to my Master. The man is out of breath and wheezing, and he smells of donkeys. "The Lady," he gasps, "says come." My Master remains seated, shrugging his shoulders in reply." "In the wagon," the man puffs. Then he tugs at my Master's sleeve. "She says 'Now!'"

My Master gets up slowly, lifts his pack, and settles it just right on his back as the man dances around him like a child who needs to pee. My Master carefully uncoils the leash and places it over my head. Only then do we set off after the little man, but he soon loses us in the crowd and has to double back to us as we amble along. We are easy to find since everyone is now backing away from the two of us, leaving us at the center of a moving empty circle.

"Please, please," the man cries, "she's so upset she's beside herself. She even threatened to have me beaten." At this my Master quickens our pace. We both know how it feels to be beaten.

As we approach the wagon I smell sickness and see Mary sitting on the ground leaning against one of the wooden wheels. Her face is pale, and there is sweat above her upper lip. My Master and I rush forward, both of us troubled for her, but Mary smiles and waves a hand in the air in front of her. "It's nothing, nothing at all," she says, but there is a bowl beside her, and the cloth that covers it cannot mask the smell of vomit. "It was just the swaying and bumping on the road, and the heat under all that felt. It's wonderful out here in the clean air, isn't it?" She holds her hand out to me and I lick it.

Her skin is healthy and pure; there is no taste of lingering illness.

The woman with the lap-dog voice calls out from inside the wagon, "Driver? Driver! Where's that worthless caravan guard? Why isn't he here yet?" My Master hands my leash to Mary and climbs up, his every motion filled with dread. If he had a tail it would be tucked between his legs.

I pay no attention to what is happening inside. Mary is right here, running her fingers through my fur, her touch soothing the raw spot where the wolf ripped out my hair. Unlike the others, she is not afraid of me. She whispers, "Hello, my beautiful friend. I missed you!"

I lick her face, which is beginning to lose its pallor. She settles herself with the back of her head resting on the top edge of the wheel, a position which does not look comfortable to me. Still, her breath is deep and steady as she gazes out at the tall stony slope rising up within sight of our stopping place. There are many spring flowers growing there on the mountainside, and her focus travels very slowly upward to the summit. It is as if each rock and blossom holds a treasure hidden inside and, one by one, she is unlocking them with her eyes. After she has reached the top she sighs and says, "What a blessing it must be to run free in the wind and sunshine, like a leaping deer in the mountain places."

She turns toward me and places her hand on my chest just below my throat where my fur is thickest, and I lean forward into her touch as I listen. "You were on my mind this morning, my friend, but I'm glad you weren't really with me. If you'd been inside the wagon there wouldn't be room for you to stand up, let alone leap. There's not a spare inch of space for any kind of movement at all. All the Lady's boxes and baskets of her things are stacked around her like the pieces of a child's puzzle. She reclines on her couch with no room for her to stand or sit. I had to crouch by her side and wait until she needed me to fetch something, food or drink or a scarf or a mirror. But I kept losing my balance because of the rough road, and it was hard to breathe since the Lady likes the feel of heat surrounding her so all the flaps are kept closed."

She grins at me as she goes on. "I tried hard to think of something else to keep my stomach from rising up, so I thought of you, out here in the daylight and the air. It helped for a while, but then... ugh!" She glances down at the covered bowl and laughs. "By God's good grace I'd just finished bathing the Lady's feet, so I was on my knees and had that basin with me. Otherwise the floor and bedding would have been a mess and the rest of her journey would have been unbearable for her."

I thump my tail on the ground in agreement with her cheerful mood, and she laughs again. Just as I start to lay my head in her lap my Master reappears and clambers down to us, calling back into the wagon as he descends. "Yes, Lady, I understand completely. For this price you will be as safe as a queen in her palace. And you can tell everyone you have King Herod's own war-dog to protect you."

By the time he arrives I am sitting at attention like the war-dog he has promised. He says to Mary, "Well, Girl, it's clear the Lady won't have you riding inside with her anymore, so we've agreed on a different plan. I can't keep you with me on my guard patrol, so you'll have to walk here beside the wagon. I'll come by each evening and pitch a small tent for you for privacy. And my fine guardian dog, Bellator, will walk by your side the whole way and sleep next to your tent. He can protect both you and the Lady at once, and no harm will come to anyone."

I am working very hard to keep my tail still. My new job is to travel next to Mary for many days, and stay by her side at night. Mary, who scratches behind my ear and talks to me in her low, sweet voice. But because I am well trained, I am able to hear this while sitting straight up without wriggling like a nursing puppy.

Mary says, "Thank you, sir, for all your kindness. I'll be happy to do as you say." I can see the glee in her eyes, although her tone is the proper one for a young girl to a grown man placed in authority over her. Then she adds, "I've never heard the name 'Bellator' before. Can you tell me what it means?"

She has asked the right question. My Master straightens up and holds his head high before he answers. "The name is Latin, the language of the Romans. It means 'warrior.' I've trained this dog myself, and I own him, I, a Nazarene like yourself. He can hunt large game or charge into battle at the stirrup of an officer or a great hero, and he'll fight as fiercely as any trusted soldier. I promised your father I'd keep you safe, and I'm keeping my word. Bellator will guard you well, and deal swift death to anyone who poses a threat. I'm bringing him to Herod's Palace in Jerusalem. Herod's own

Master of the Hunt saw my Bellator in action last month in Sephoris and placed the order on the spot. After the king himself gave his approval I was sent an official contract and my directions for delivery."

Mary smiles and responds in a fitting formal tone, "It will be a great honor to travel in the company of such a remarkable creature. Thank you, sir. Thank you very much."

My Master is clearly pleased with himself. He bows in our direction and then turns and strolls off to join his comrades. All of his problems are solved, including the new difficulty of patrolling with me by his side since I am the cause of so much anger. And on top of his wages as a guard he has also secured extra payments from Mary's father and the Lady. My Master has a plan, and all the money he makes helps him to carry it out. I may be a warrior, but when it comes to both tactics and long-term strategy my Master is the true champion.

Chapter 5

Now that my Master has left I can finally lay my head in Mary's lap. She is just placing her hand on the back of my neck when the thin little driver jumps from his seat to the ground beside us. He stands looking down at us, wringing his hands and nodding his head like a bird pecking at a bug. I am tempted to growl and scare him away, but instead Mary speaks to him. "Oh Ethan, thank you so much for your kindness this morning. I felt so much better riding up front with you with in the fresh air after what happened inside." If he is Mary's friend I cannot very well frighten him now.

"Pardon me, Miss," he says. "It may not be my place to speak, but ..." He swallows rapidly three times, and I watch with interest as the little lump on the front of his neck bobs up and down before he resumes speaking. "After what everyone's been saying, do you think that animal is, well... safe? And besides, aren't dogs unclean?"

Mary laughs, not the mocking laughter of the army camp, but softly, like a good friend sharing a joke. "Oh Ethan, Bellator is a beautiful creature sent into my life by the hand of the Lord himself, to be my companion. This dog would never harm us. He's our protector. Come here, put you hand on his head. You'll see."

The man takes a step forward. I can see that he trusts Mary more than he fears me, so I allow him to come near. My head is still on Mary's lap, and I can feel the touch on my forehead of one shaking finger before the man jerks it as far away from my mouth as he can get it. Then to my great surprise a small smile creeps onto his face and he reaches out again and places the whole palm of his hand on my head.

"His fur is so soft," he says, and he begins to move his hand back and forth in a motion that feels wonderful. But he ruins it all by adding, "It's as soft as the nose of a donkey's new colt."

I snap my head up and the man jumps back, but Mary says, "Bellator, I hope we can all be kind to one another on this long journey."

The little man, Ethan, laughs. "He's got spirit, Miss, I don't mind that a bit. We can all be friends, eh, Boy?" So I wag my tail instead of growling. As I said, we dogs do not chew over old insults.

But Mary says, "Bellator, when you're here by my side you're more than a warrior. You're also a reminder of how our Lord provides for us and sends us surprises every moment of every day. So I'm going to call you 'Tobias', because it means 'God is good.'

"Tobias," repeats the little man named Ethan. "That's a nice name. I once had a donkey named Toby." I am tempted again to growl, but he reaches down, picks up the basin from the ground and says, "I don't think you'll be needing this anymore, Miss, so I'll just go empty it and clean it out." Because my head is on her lap I can feel Mary start to gather her muscles to stand, but Ethan insists, "No, please, just rest and maybe close your eyes for a while. That beast of yours is practically asleep, so let's not disturb him. You both have a long walk ahead of you, as much as ten more miles before evening." Since he is taking good care of Mary that means he is my friend, so there will be no more thoughts of growling.

Chapter 6

After he leaves, Mary bends over me and whispers in my ear, "Oh Tobias, feeling so sick has lit such joy in me, and I have to say it out loud to someone. I think it's a sign to assure me that what the angel said is true."

Angel? I love angels. My Master and his rabbi friend sit and talk about them for hours. Since I have never seen one I have trouble with the exact meaning of the word, but all the wonder and excitement in their voices always makes me tremble. So as Mary speaks softly close to my ear, I can feel a tremor run from my nose to my tail.

"I was asleep two nights ago," she continues, "there on the floor of our house. My mat was between my parents like it always is, and when I opened my eyes in the darkness at first I thought my mother was singing in her sleep. Then the sound grew, and it was all around me and inside me, and there were no limits to the depth or the wideness of it. All the music in the world was coming to me at once, and at the same time it seemed as if the stars and the earthen floor and my own soul were all humming together like the strings of a lyre. I sat up and pulled my knees under me, and as soon as I was kneeling suddenly there was light, first one point like white fire hanging in the air, then a glow that lit every corner of the room, and everywhere it touched my skin it felt like warm honey. The light formed into a column right in front of me and the music became a voice, and the voice sang a greeting to me with meanings instead of words, joy and a sense of great blessings filling me up and overflowing, and God present to me with no veil of separation until my awe was so deep that I began to shake. Then the voice spoke and said, "Do not be afraid," and suddenly I knew it was an angel, a messenger of the Lord, and I knew no harm would come to me."

As Mary whispers to me I can follow her feelings as strongly as her words, and what she says about the angel makes me want to leap up and bark and run in circles, but I remain perfectly still, although not with the tense stillness of a war-dog poised for action. Perhaps being with Mary is teaching me to quiet myself in a different way so I can be a good companion for her.

"Oh Tobias," she murmurs, "I need to keep repeating the angel's message to be sure every part of it stays clear and solid in my memory, and nothing gets lost. I need to get ready for what's coming, since it's not what I've been expecting until now. For a long time I've been promised to a good man named Joseph, but we're not married yet. I'm still a young girl, a virgin living under her parents' roof. But the angel said I am going to have a baby.

"I asked the angel how I could be a mother since I've never been with a man, and again there were meanings rather than words, the unveiled presence of the Spirit of God and a holiness so wild and boundless that all questions melted into one great Amen, and I answered, "Let it be done." And now I carry the Son of the Most High inside me, here under my heart, right where your nice warm head is resting.

"This little child will grow up to be a king. And not just any king, Tobias. He's going to restore the great throne of King David, and his kingdom will never end. In less than a year the One our God has promised throughout the ages will be born, and I will be his mother. The angel even gave me the name to call him: Jesus. It means 'God saves'.

"This baby will come into the world through me because God is reaching right into our lives and saving us, and all this is happening now. I'm still just Mary, the same girl I was last week, nothing more. But now I know I've been chosen to serve my God and my people in a way I never even imagined."

Mary sighs and my head rises and falls with her breath. "At least this is what I believe, with my whole heart and soul and mind and strength," she says. "But when I woke my parents up to tell them about it, they said they never heard or saw a thing and it was all a dream.

"Of course, I didn't give up trying. The angel also told me my mother's kinswoman Elizabeth has been carrying a child of her own for six months now, even though she's much too old for childbearing. I told my mother this while she was lighting the morning cook-fire in the courtyard, and she just laughed. But then I told her one more thing the angel said: 'Nothing is impossible for God.'

"When my mother heard this she made me sit down beside her on the bench by the fire and tell her everything again from the beginning, and then she took me in her arms. 'Could this be true?' she said. 'Could the Lord have chosen you out of all the generations of our people, my own good warm-hearted daughter? You've always been such a treasure to me,' she said, smoothing back the hair at my temple with such a tender touch that I felt like a little girl again. 'Maybe I'm not just a prideful mother blind to the flaws of her own child. Maybe the Lord God sees you as I do. Maybe every day of your life you've been on your own graceful pathway with each step and movement carrying you toward this moment. Has God been preparing you for this from the beginning? It is certainly not impossible, and that's enough to start with.'

"So my mother and I formed a plan. If Elizabeth is really six months pregnant, that will be proof to my parents that the angel was real and the whole message is true. So if I go to Judea and visit our cousin and see her condition for myself, then that will be that, one way or the other. And my mother said if it's true, then this journey will put me right where I need to be to help Elizabeth when she'll need help the most. My mother is a very practical woman.

"But, oh, Tobias, my father was a different story. He said 'No, no, no,' all that day," and with each 'no' Mary gives my head a firm pat. "No rush to disrupt all our lives for what was probably just a dream, no need for a journey when we can send a message to Elizabeth and wait patiently for an answer, and, most of all, no visit from an angel unless it was confirmed by long and careful discussions with the rabbi and the village elders.

"That evening at the table all through our Shabbat prayer and supper he was stiff and formal with us, but the next morning after he came out of the synagogue and chatted with some friends he joined us on the walk home with his shoulders slumped and head bowed. 'Well, Anna,' he said, "Jacob for no particular reason told me the son of my old friend Samuel, whose memory I honor, is leaving with a caravan tomorrow morning for Judea. Then who should walk up to us but Samuel's son himself. This could not just be a coincidence coming on a Shabbat after the morning service, on a day when we always remember the great journey of Moses and our people. I could not spit in the face of God, so I gave in and asked my old friend's son if he would be willing to escort Mary to Elizabeth and Zechariah's house for us. I was hoping he'd just say 'No' and end the whole thing, but instead he agreed to do it. I still think our Mary's too young for such a long journey without us, and I still think this whole thing was just a dream. However, I have made my decision. I am going to allow her to go. But only if you can have everything she needs ready before dawn without breaking the Shabbat in even the smallest way with your preparations.'

"My mother and I had already packed my things the day before, so that meant the answer was 'yes'. After sundown as soon as the three stars appeared in the sky and the Shabbat was over my father left for the home of Samuel's son since they still had to make the business arrangements for the trip. That was something that couldn't be done on the Lord's Day. While he was gone I bathed myself and we washed and braided my hair. Just like that, I was ready. My mother even had time to run to her friend Rachel the weaver's house and get a soft little wool blanket as a gift for Elizabeth's baby. I have it here in my bundle.

"We all laid ourselves down early last night, although I didn't sleep much. My mind and soul were still ringing with the angel's music, as if I myself were a psalm to the Lord. But I'm not tired at all today. And when I was sick this morning all I could think of was my mother's friends complaining about feeling the same way when they were expecting babies, so each heave of my stomach seemed like part of the song. Not as much fun as being visited by an angel, of course, but still a part of the whole."

Mary stops whispering and moves back into her stillness. After a few moments her breathing tells me she's fallen asleep, so I close my eyes, too. For dogs, this is one of our favorite pass-times. Sometimes we sleep, but often we just lie here being aware of all that surrounds us, letting the smells and the sounds and the feel of the earth beneath our bodies soothe us. It always makes us happy, but now Mary is here with me and it is more than happiness. I have no word for it.

I do not understand much of what Mary just told me, but I do know the meaning of 'child', 'baby' and 'mother', and if Mary is sure there was an angel then I am sure, too. I keep my senses alert while she sleeps, pleased to have a task I can perform for her.

Little by little I can hear the caravan coming back to life after its rest time. I open my eyes as Ethan comes near and puts his hand on Mary's shoulder. "Before we get moving, Miss, I brought you something to keep your strength up." He hands Mary a small bowl and pours the water for her hand washing, and when she is done he proudly presents a plate of dates and cheese arranged on top of a disc of flat bread. The dates have an unexpected scent of cinnamon. He has a cup of water for her in his other hand. Mary says, "Ethan, you're so good to me! Thank you very much."

But Ethan isn't done. After Mary prays a blessing over her meal he reaches into his pocket and brings out another hunk of cheese, which he holds out in front of me. I love cheese! But there is hardly ever any left over after people's meals so I rarely get a taste of it except for the times my Master brings me to the wedding feast of one or another of his many cousins. Then I watch from a distance until late in the evening after everyone has had many cups of wine. This is when my Master always brings me a napkin bulging with the bits of cheese that were left over.

The piece of cheese Ethan is now holding is not even old and dried out. It is fresh and moist and my nose twitches with pleasure. I take it with a gentle mouth, careful not to show my teeth as I gulp it down. Ethan has done me a great honor by offering both the cheese and his naked hand, and I will not forget.

After the cheese I bend down to drink the water in Mary's washing-bowl, which is even better than licking her hand. It is delicious, but when I look up with water dripping from my jowls both Mary and Ethan are laughing at me. There is so much that humans will never understand.

Mary does not eat her meal the same way I ate my cheese. In fact, if she were among either war-dogs or soldiers she would probably be hungry all the time since there are always those who will fall on any uneaten food and devour it, even if it is in someone else's dish. For this reason dogs and soldiers learn to eat quickly.

However, Mary does not do this very sensible thing even though there is a large dog beside her who might not be trustworthy around an unguarded plate. Instead she breaks off a small piece of bread, wraps it around just one of the dates, and places it in her mouth. Next she closes her eyes and smiles as she slowly chews this morsel. When she has swallowed it she looks at Ethan and says, "I've never tasted anything so wonderful before. The cinnamon turns both the bread and the date into something new. Thank you so much for sharing this with me, Ethan."

As she continues with her meal I begin to wonder what my cheese would have been like if I had eaten it Mary's slow and careful way.

When her food is gone I watch Mary pray again. We dogs do not pray. We have no need to remind ourselves that we are creatures and our lives are not our own. Instead we are born and we die knowing our part in the great and satisfying dance of all things. In spite of this we do not mock humans when they pray. We respect their need to struggle just to approach what we were given as a gift. It is not their fault. It is the only way for them to find their own place in the dance.

Chapter 7

Mary is back in her silence, so there are no words as we travel side by side enjoying the spring afternoon. She has the long easy stride of a country girl who walks wherever she wants to go, not like the mincing steps of the women who parade around the army camp trailing their smells of sweat and musk and perfume.

Mary's right hand is touching the ruff of fur on the back of my neck. Some people say this is my mane because I look like a brown lion, but I have never seen a lion and I have never seen myself so I do not know if this is true. She has tied my leather leash loosely around her waist so both hands can swing freely at her sides. I must remember not to chase anything suddenly or I will pull her off her feet. I hope nothing threatens us before my Master can come and correct her understandable ignorance of war-dog handling. But perhaps she is protected by her angel and does not need me. I keep watching the space around her carefully, but in the bright afternoon sunshine I can see no column of white fire and I do not know the scent of angels. Because of this it is hard to tell.

For me this footpace makes for an easy day. I am trained to run for many hours at a time to keep up with a troop of cavalry, so I have not even begun to tire when shadows lengthen. The fading light allows just a glimpse of white stone towers on a hilltop rising in the distance, so we must be near Scythopolis. As dusk falls visibility begins to favor any robbers lying in ambush, and I become tense with attention. Finally a shouted command is passed along and the caravan comes to a disorderly halt.

Mary and I wait by the wagon as Ethan climbs down from his high seat. He is stiff from long sitting so this takes some time. Unlike dogs, people do not know how to lower their forequarters and stretch their spines when they get up. When he finally reaches the ground Mary says, "Now it's your turn to rest while I fix a meal for you and the Lady."

But Ethan shakes his head and answers, "Oh now, Miss, I've been planning this supper all day. In my traveling days I picked up the habit of having a real meal at the end of work, something to look forward to, if you know what I mean. I started my lentils in hot water at last night's cook-fire, and they've been soaking all day up there in the space under the seat. That's my kitchen, you see. Then there's the loaf of yeast bread I've been proofing all afternoon. I have some nice cardamom and herbs all ready, and some lovely onions and carrots. And I saved some of that cheese your beast's so fond of."

Mary touches his arm and says, "Why, Ethan, what a bundle of surprises you are to me. Let me watch you cook so I can learn some of your skills." Now there is such a smile on the man's face that he lights up like a candle in a cave.

Mary and I settle down on the ground as he unhitches and tends to the donkeys, again refusing Mary's offer of help. He also brings me some water in a bowl of my own, which I drink carefully, without wasting a drop. He has carried this water for me and I am thankful.

While I am drinking he reaches up under the front of the wagon seat and unfastens a wooden flap that folds down into a shelf. From beneath the seat he brings out a dirty cloth sack and a black iron pot with a hollow chamber built in underneath it. Instead of a regular lid the pot has an iron box that fits on top and covers most of the opening. A small lid fits over the remaining space. He takes a handful of charcoal out of the bag, puts it in a basket made of metal strips, and lights a twisted bunch of twigs under it with a spark from a flint. He next lifts down a clay pot reeking of yeast. Then there's a wooden chest with a rich mixture of scents that makes me sneeze three times in a row, so of course they both laugh at me again.

Ethan puts the basket of glowing charcoals inside the lower chamber of his iron cooker, punches down the bread and places it into the box on the top, and then stirs some powder from the wooden chest into the contents of the pot, which smell of wet lentils. He says, "Miss, if you'll slice the carrots into nice thin strips and cut the little onions in half, our work will be done."

As Mary does as he asked she says, "I've never seen anything like your iron pot and chest of spices before, or your wagon, either. Will you tell me where they came from?" Mary knows how to ask people good questions about themselves, and she also knows how to listen to their answers without interrupting to talk about herself. This is unusual in humans.

Ethan settles down beside us and begins to speak.

"It's a long story, Miss. I was poor as a boy. In fact I grew up in the south in the same village as the Lady. We played together as children, although I'm sure she doesn't remember me. Even then she was always far above me. As a child Rebekah was known throughout Judea as a beauty. When she was 14 her parents betrothed her to a rich merchant who'd just buried his third wife, all of them dead in childbirth and he with no children to leave his fortune to. So she went away with him and bore him two fine sons.

"I was restless and had some ambition, so since my parents knew Rebekah's family I built up my courage and went to the merchant to ask for a job on one of his caravans. I watched and learned as I traveled far and wide, just like you learned by watching me cook. I saved my wages instead of drinking or gambling them away, and I started to buy my own goods, especially spices. They were no burden to carry and very easy and profitable to sell. I had to test the quality of my purchases so I learned to cook. The pot is from a blacksmith who traveled with us for a year. I designed it myself for long stretches of road with no firewood since it uses very little fuel. The smith put together the parts for me from a pot and a box and some scraps for the bottom chamber." Ethan looks at the ground and the color of his face deepens. He is embarrassed as good humans sometimes are when they catch themselves speaking of their own accomplishments.

He continues, "Eventually I had enough saved up to buy this wagon from a Scythian friend who was getting too old for life on the road. He was a big man who told stories from all over the world. He had a laugh like the bellow of a bull, and a wagon that looked like the nest of a rat. He kept all his goods in a jumble inside, and even though he knew exactly where everything was it took him forever to unearth what he wanted. As soon as the wagon was mine and my old friend was gone I fitted every inch out with shelves and hooks so I'd never miss a good trade by making a customer wait too long. But my favorite part is my little kitchen under the seat. All my cooking things fit into compartments, and I can eat like a king every morning and every night.

Mary smiles and nods her head, which makes Ethan blush again. After all the bragging in the army camp I am drawn to his shy manner. Mary chooses her friends wisely.

He continues, "As the years went by the merchant saw how much I'd learned and in time he sent his two sons, one after the other, to travel with me in my wagon so they could watch and learn, too. They both went on to do very well.

"Then last year I decided I'd traveled enough and had money enough, so it was time for me to leave the caravan road. I bought a farm near Capernaum with a comfortable little house, my own garden for vegetables, a barn for some chickens and my donkeys, a small grape arbor, a few date palms, and best of all three olive trees, ancient and twisted and, well, beautiful. We'll have some oil I pressed myself with our bread tonight." Mary claps her hands with delight.

His face darkens with embarrassment again, but this time he keeps his head up as Mary says, "But if you live so happily on your farm now, what brings you and your wagon on this journey?"

"Ah, Miss, that's the sad part of the story. Two years ago the old merchant died after a long illness. Last month I had a message from his younger son, Benjamin. The old man passed away at his summer home on the shore of the Sea of Galilee, near this very caravan road. That's the house Benjamin inherited. Jacob now owns the bigger house near where the trade routes intersect at Bethlehem. Rebekah stayed in Galilee with Benjamin after her husband died, but after two years her son and his wife decided she'd go to Jacob's home for a while. She wanted to bring all her belongings with her, so the two sons thought of me and wondered if I'd kept my wagon after I settled down. I told them I'd be happy to transport their mother and her things in gratitude for all their family had done for me so many years ago. So here I am, and having a fine time, although I must say my donkeys don't seem very pleased to be back on the job."

I look over at the four donkeys as they stuff themselves with grass by the wayside. Their sides are fat, and hauling the heavy wagon will do them no harm. Romans believe in constant training and exercise, but clearly these are not Roman donkeys.

Mary thanks Ethan for his story and starts to ask him more about his travels, but I look past the donkeys and see my Master coming. He whistles and I jump up, ready to go. Mary still has the leash around her waist, and my Master laughs as he approaches. He calls out, "Well, Girl, that's a good way to get yourself dragged down the road like a chariot." He is still laughing; he is not scolding her. My Master is in a good mood.

Mary returns his cheerful tone as she unties the leather strap. "Does he really need a leash at all, Sir? He's so well trained I can't imagine him running away."

"You're right," he answers. "No more leash. It's really just to show people in crowds that he's under control and not about to run wild and start ripping their arms off for his supper. Since he's nearly the size of a small pony people can get very nervous around him. But he's surely taken to you, Girl. Want to help me run him through his paces?"

Mary looks toward Ethan, who says, "Please go ahead, Miss. We won't eat for another hour or so, and there's nothing left to do but wait."

Chapter 8

Head up, I wait for the signal. My Master points his whole hand and arm toward the wheat field beside the road and I launch myself at full speed, glad to be free of the leash and ready to show Mary what I can do.

I run the full length and breadth of the four sides of the field, establishing a perimeter and alert for everything I can see, smell, hear or feel as I race along. We are called sight-hounds, we war-dogs, because our vision is clearer and longer than many lesser breeds who need to cast about with their noses to the ground to find anything at all, even an elephant. What use would their noses be in a battle? To see the coming blow, duck and parry and attack the weak spot, all this takes the eye and speed and heart of a superior animal.

I know this because I myself am a superior animal, not a lesser breed. I am a Molossus, and we are famous. I once heard Claudius tell my Master that the owners of some of the finest homes in Rome announce loudly that their houses are protected by a Molossus, even when there are no dogs of any kind inside. Our name alone is enough to make any street criminal turn tail and run like a wet cat. Claudius is known throughout the Roman army for producing and training the best dogs in all the lands east of Rome, and he and my Master send my Molossi kin out to every legion in our sector. Since I am first among Claudius' war-dogs, I am chosen to sire more pups than any other member of our pack. At the memory of this very enjoyable honor I toss my head as I complete my initial run.

I return to my Master and sit to show there is no threat in my area. Squirrels, a badger sett, the day-old track of a small bear, many mice, and best of all, a sprawling rabbit warren. My Master says, "Hungry, boy? Work first, then you can hunt."

I love drills. I follow every command instantly, even when my Master tries to trick me with two orders on top of each other, or when he turns his back to see if I will keep doing what he signaled or said even without his watchful eye upon me. Several times he sends me to run the perimeter, but even late in the drill when he sends me twice with no pause in between my speed never slackens. The rabbits are used to me now and venture out into the wheat for a last nibble before full darkness, but I ignore them.

Finally my Master gives the last signal: Hunt! The rabbits were not wise to ignore me, and I have three of them down, necks snapped and ready to eat, before the rest of the poor stupid animals notice what's happening and scurry underground. They are meant to be caught just as I am meant to catch them.

I collect my kill and trot back to my Master, but instead of placing them at his feet I proudly drop them in front of Mary. Too late, I see the expression on her face. She does not realize I have honored her. Instead she looks away from the dead rabbits with distress in her eyes.

My Master says, "I wonder why he did that? He's trained to bring everything he's hunted to me. Before he eats anything he has to wait for my permission. That way he'll never forget that all his food comes from my hand."

Mary places the palm of one hand on her belly, and she is smiling at me with the same smile she had when she was talking about the angel. "Good dog," she says. She places her other arm around my neck and kisses me on my nose. "Good, good dog. You know exactly where everything that we have comes from, and who to thank. You've brought me another sign."

My Master is still shaking his head and muttering as he carries my three rabbits out to the far side of the field so I can enjoy them in private without troubling anyone. People of the faith of my Master and Mary and Ethan avoid rabbit and squirrel and some of my other favorite foods, so I do not eat these things in front of them. Besides, this kind of meal can be very messy, although my Master helps by slitting the rabbits open from chin to crotch before he puts them down on the ground. I sit and wait until he gives me his signal. Then I feast.

Chapter 9

It takes me a while to lick the remains of the rabbits from my paws and muzzle, and by the time I get back to the wagon Mary, Ethan and my Master are finished with their supper, too. As soon as Ethan sees me he jumps up and brings me my promised hunk of cheese, and my tail swings to thank him for remembering. It is delicious! I think humans call this 'dessert.'

Mary climbs up past Ethan's empty seat and disappears into the darkness inside the thick felt cave, but I do not whine because now I know she will return. Soon she comes back with the Lady's empty plate as the two men unroll a bundle of striped cloth that is attached to the side panel of the wagon between the two wheels. They fit some wooden rods together and prop them under the cloth, and all of a sudden there is a small tent beside the wagon. We dogs do not fit rods together to make things so I do not know how this was done, but I know it takes much longer for a trained Roman soldier to set up a tent, and so does my Master. He is hitting Ethan on the shoulder the way men do with their friends, and Ethan is looking at the ground again, being what I think is called humble.

Mary has brought her sack of belongings down from the wagon, and at the entrance of her little tent Ethan hands her a rolled-up rug. Suddenly everyone is saying "Good night" and moving in different directions, Mary into the tent, my Master off to his post and Ethan toward the place where he has tethered his beloved donkeys. I stand in the moonlight, unsure of just where I am meant to be. This is when Mary opens the tent-flap and says, "There. The rug is in place and my sleeping mat is unrolled. Now you can come inside, Tobias."

Inside! I will sleep beside Mary inside her private tent. She says, "It'll be a tight fit, but I'm used to sleeping between my parents. It will be such a comfort to have you here, showing me I'm not alone. I know God is always with us, but still it's good to feel and hear the breath of someone who cares about you when you wake up in the dark."

As she readies herself for sleep I wonder if the angel is in here with us, too, along with Mary and God and myself. This tent must be bigger than it looked from the outside. Just as Mary settles in beside me with her hand resting on my neck, the sound of a single voice comes to us, singing high and sweet:

"I will sing of the LORD's great love forever;
with my mouth I will make your faithfulness known
through all generations.
I will declare that your love
stands firm forever,
that you have established your faithfulness
in heaven itself.
You said, "I have made a covenant with my chosen one,
I have sworn to David my servant,
'I will establish your line forever
and make your throne firm
through all generations." [iii]

In the silence that follows, Mary sighs deeply. I wonder if this was the voice of her angel, but she says, "Oh Tobias, so many signs have come to me in just one day. Ethan sang to me this morning when I was feeling so sick, nonsense songs people use to cheer up little children, so I knew he had a beautiful voice. But I'd forgotten that Ethan was also the name of a singer in King David's court. Our own Ethan just sang the Psalm of Ethan the Ezrahite. Did you hear it, Tobias? Even though he doesn't know anything about my secret, our friend sang about what the angel told me. 'I have sworn to David my servant, I will establish your line forever and make your throne firm through all generations.' Did you hear it, Tobias? Love, faithfulness, forever, heaven: these words are so full of truth and wonder. And now the Lord God has made me a part of this beautiful psalm."

There is silence again, and I know she is praying. Then her breathing settles into sleep and I let my eyes close. I rest, but I also remain on watch. I am part of Ethan's song now, too, because it is my job to be sure no harm comes to her. I do not understand 'forever' or 'heaven'. But 'love' and 'faithfulness' are both the same thing, and we dogs know them well.

DAY TWO

"The signs and wonders that the Most High God has worked for me I am pleased to recount."

Daniel 4:2 [iv]

Chapter 10

In the morning before her own breakfast Mary climbs up to bring the Lady her morning washing water and help her with what women do when they wake up. The camp is still quiet, and I can hear most of their words. The Lady asks, "What was that lovely singing last night?", and Mary tells her it was Ethan. Then the woman says, with the pitch of her voice rising to a fearful whine, "Ethan? Ethan! And just who is Ethan? Did you have a stranger here with you last night, hiding in the darkness right next to my wagon?"

Mary does not explain that men who are hiding in darkness do not sing. Instead she says Ethan is the name of the Lady's driver, and adds, "Maybe you remember him from your parents' village. You played together when you were children."

Now the lap-dog voice snaps, "That's ridiculous! I was never allowed to play with servants. Now go and fetch my breakfast."

Ethan is walking toward us from his sleeping-place by the donkeys with his rolled-up bedding tucked under his arm, so I do not think he heard what the Lady said. Well before dawn I heard him beside the wagon quietly opening and closing his iron pot-lid, and now from the scent of it the boiled cracked wheat is ready to serve. Mary tells him how beautiful his Psalm was last night, and instead of looking at the ground Ethan meets her eye and smiles, saying, "Thank you, Miss. My voice is a gift from the Lord. My father was a singer, and he prayed before I was born for a child who could sing along with him. My four older brothers carry a tune a bit like my donkeys would. My father named me Ethan to give the Lord a little nudge, since Ethan sang for King David himself. Names were very important to my dad."

Mary nods and says, "I think God would be pleased to have you yourself sing for a great king, my friend." As she turns away to reach for the empty plates she winks at me, and I wonder if babies inside their mothers can really hear sounds like music. Then she adds, "And names are important to me, too. I was named for Miriam the sister of Moses, so if you remember to call me 'Mary', I promise to think of her dancing with her tambourine every time you sing."

He laughs and says, "I do love the sound of a nice tambourine… Mary."

Ethan is busy spooning out the breakfast when Mary adds, "Rebekah also says your singing last night was lovely."

Now his smile fades and his hands stop moving. A dollop of porridge drops off his spoon onto the ground and I wait, looking hard at the fallen food so close to my paw. Mary moves her hand like my Master and says, "Tobias, it's yours," and as I grab it with my mouth, dirt and all, she and Ethan share another laugh at my expense. Ethan pulls out a wooden bowl, fills it up, and sets it on the ground by his side. While I wait, Mary turns her back to me and steps in front of Ethan. Then she moves away and Ethan gives me the "go" hand sign. He says, "Tobias, it's yours." He has learned my signal, given me my own bowl and served me my own breakfast. He is definitely my friend.

The caravan is more orderly this morning and we move out much earlier. Things are not up to Roman standards, of course, but with so many women, children and uncooperative donkeys I do not expect much. As we walk Mary wears her silence like the wick of a lamp wears the light. It surrounds her and moves with her and brings brightness to everything it touches. But at this moment a sharp noise breaks in, a shouted word, "Hey!" Mary and I look behind us and see a thin-faced young man approaching. His garment is richly woven, but it is wrinkled and stained and smells of old gravy.

He falls in on Mary's right, pushing a stream of words through his mouth in a torrent as he arrives. "You're the girl who's traveling alone, right?" It is not a real question because he does not pause for an answer. "I thought you might need some company. I can tell you all the news. I'm with the leader of the whole caravan so I always know what's going on. You can ask me anything about anybody." Mary does not ask him anything, but he continues anyway. "I can tell you who's having a fight, who's trying to cheat somebody on a trade deal, who's sneaking into someone else's campsite at night, who's stealing supplies- nobody puts anything past me." While he talks I focus on his face. His mouth is moving rapidly and his eyes are watching Mary the way a fox watches a chicken in a pen.

The young man keeps talking and talking. "I keep the accounts for the caravan. My father had me trained as a Scribe, but that was his idea of a life, not mine. Who wants to be stuck in the temple precinct trailing along after a bunch of boring old men who talk about commandments and rules all the time? But I thought some part of the training might be useful to me, and I was right, because they taught me to work with numbers. I wanted to travel, see the world, get around, and here I am. Everybody hates to do their own accounting, so I go wherever I want and work when I feel like it."

I am thinking his father should have put him in the Roman army to learn some discipline when I notice a change in his tone. "So, um, I know from the caravan leader that he just made the man you're traveling with the head of the guards this morning, and since your companion will be very busy you'll hardly be seeing him at all. So, um, here you are, a girl on your own, no father or brother or husband to tell you what to do. So, um, how about having a little fun?"

He starts to move his face toward her as he reaches over to grab Mary's arm above her elbow, but before his fingers can close I slip around her and put my body between them, shoving him with my shoulder in a maneuver invented to turn aside a charging cavalry horse. As he falls I lean over him with my teeth bared and a growl as fierce as a battle-cry. I am only trying to scare him, as I would a belligerent puppy. From the start I could tell by his smell that he is harmless. He is also as stupid as a puppy. He said he always knows what is going on, but he never noticed that Mary had a giant Molossus war-dog walking by her side.

Still on his back, he scuttles away from me like the little freshwater crabs on the beach at Capernaum. It is amusing to watch, although I continue my growling. When he has moved to what he thinks is a safe distance he scrambles to his feet and tries to run, but his long legs wobble and he needs to put a hand back on the ground to support himself. As he finally turns and races away there is a fresh wet stain down the back of his robe, along with a streak the color of mud. This whole thing may not be a story he chooses to tell to others.

This time there is a witness to my triumph more reliable than the boy I saved from the wolves. This time my story will be told. For this reason I am excited as I turn to Mary, but her voice calms me down as she speaks. "Dear Tobias, I don't know whether to laugh or cry. I'm very thankful for your protection, but that poor young man was such a sad figure. Maybe if I'd been able to talk to him I might have helped. It must cripple your soul to see everyone on earth as boring or greedy or dishonest. Think of his father, longing for a son who wants to serve the Lord and ending up with someone who only seems to care about his own pleasures. I don't think he was really going to hurt me, but when someone says his world is so centered on himself it's hard to know where he'd stop or what would stop him." She puts her hand on my head and I lean it toward her as we walk along. "Well, I guess that's not true. You certainly knew what would stop him, Tobias, and since the Lord sent you that probably means he needed some stopping." Mary is running her fingers in small circles behind my ear as she speaks, so it is hard to concentrate on her words. She said she is thankful, and that the Lord sent me. I do not need to solve any puzzles about the annoying young man now that he has run away.

Mary says "Let's go walk closer to Ethan." We have been trailing behind the wagon, away from the pungent effect of the morning sun on the hides of the sweating donkeys. Now Mary runs forward and I follow until we are next to Ethan's high seat. She calls out a greeting to Ethan and he smiles and waves at her, but it would be hard for them to talk to each other above the noise of the wheels and the hooves and the creaking harnesses. She does not climb up to tell Ethan about the young man and my heroic rescue. Instead Mary returns to her silence, but her face is troubled, the same way she looked when she talked about the annoying young man. I wonder if she is thinking about him as she prays. I wonder if she is even praying for him.

Chapter 11

We stop for our mid-day break, but Mary does not tell Ethan about my bravery and today there is no cheese. Still, Ethan gives me a big crust of yesterday's yeast bread soaked in olive oil so I am content to drowse beside them in the sun as they eat olives and almonds with their own bread.

Suddenly the sun is gone and a wind is stirring up the dust on the road and driving dark clouds over our heads. Ethan gathers our things and stows them in the wagon just as the rain begins to pelt down on us. He opens a canvas awning over his high seat and pulls Mary up to ride beside him. They are both hidden from my sight and I am alone on the ground with the donkeys as the wagon starts to lumber along through the mud. I cannot see or hear or smell Mary, but I am not distressed as I trot beside the wagon in the cooling rain. She is safe up there with Ethan, and we war-dogs are accustomed to performing our daily drills in every kind of weather. We march. We do not complain like low-ranking foot-soldiers as mile follows mile.

When the sun returns it is hanging low in the sky, so a good part of the afternoon is gone without much progress in our journey. I am having a good long shake to shed many pounds of water from my sodden coat when Ethan stops the wagon for a moment and Mary jumps down. She laughs and holds her hands in front of her to protect herself from the flying droplets. Still laughing, she says, "Tobias, with all your fur fluffed out like that you look like a big fuzzy bear." Even though I am still wet she puts her arms around my neck and hugs me. "I'm sorry there was no room for my poor soaked guardian up under the shelter," she says, and I wag my tail even though the thought of a Roman army dog cowering away from a little rain like a housecat would normally be an insult.

The storm that crossed our path has blown itself away from us, leaving nothing behind but a soft breeze smelling of wet grasses. As Mary walks by my side her gaze is fixed on a point in the sky ahead, and when I follow the line of her sight I see a single cloud hovering in the wide expanse of blue the pale color of Mary's veil.

I do not detect anything of interest about this cloud. It is the kind that looks like an entire flock of white sheep piled in a heap and, like sheep, it poses no threat. It is not moving swiftly, so it does not tell anything about another approaching storm. It is not dark, so there is no lightning hidden within it. This is not the sort of cloud my Master would study. However, Mary's steady focus seems to be pulling her deep into the center of the whiteness as she strides along beside me.

I have seen Mary looking like this before, looking at the flowers on the mountainside this morning, looking at the branch of a tree above our campsite, looking at a hawk hovering on the wind just before the storm overtook us. I am proud of my own ability to pay attention. I can remain motionless with my eyes on the entrance to a rabbit-hole, or on my Master's hand as I wait for a command, or on an enemy battle-line as I seek a sign of forward movement during a training drill. But when I do these things I am staring at something for the purpose of getting what I want: a fat rabbit, a training task well done, the honor of being the warrior quickest to leap forward into the fray.

Mary does not want to use this cloud for anything. When she looks in this way, she seems to enter inside what she is looking at. I know this because she has looked at me in this manner, and when my eyes looked back at her I saw nothing but her gaze, not measuring me or commanding me or calculating my worth, just herself there in front of me, looking, seeing me.

Soon the late afternoon journey is over. We make camp early so people can light fires and dry their wet clothing before the chill of nightfall sets in. I am proud to see my Master approaching with his cape still dripping, as undaunted as a disciplined leader should be. After he tells us about his promotion and receives the praise that is his due he calls me to his side. To my joy Mary joins us on our walk toward a meadow lying by the roadside. Puddles and mud do not slow me as I race around the perimeter, and the deep breath of running fills me with the fresh scent of the animals who are starting to venture out into the weak sunlight.

After I run through my paces I expect the command to hunt, but instead my Master and Mary are sitting down side by side on a large flat rock. I am happy to see them settling in to talk to each other, because now it must be time for her to tell the story of how I rescued her from the man who tried to grab her arm. But when Mary speaks, she asks my Master,

"How did you come to be the owner of such a magnificent dog?"

Again, she has asked a good question. I settle at their feet on the damp earth, ready to listen to my Master talk about me.

Chapter 12

"It all started because I was born a second son," my Master says. This story does not seem to be about me after all, but I cock my ears and listen to him carefully anyway. "My twin brother beat me into this world by just a few minutes, and that's all it took.

"You already know that my father owns a large vineyard in the countryside about two miles from your own house, Girl. That's where I grew up. I can remember our two fathers sitting in the shade under our arbor and talking long into the summer afternoons over their cups of wine.

"My brother and I spent every moment of our childhood together, racing, wrestling, quarreling, playing tricks, and lying side by side in the sun eating grapes and talking about everything young boys find to talk about. We had no secrets from each other- or so I thought.

"Then one morning when my brother and I were 10 our father took us up on the hill behind the house and pointed out all the boundaries of our property. He said, 'Our family lands were kept intact by my father and grandfather and his father before him because the oldest son has always inherited everything.' Then my father turned to me and said, 'And you, Jeremiah? What trade would you like to learn so you can make your way in the world? Or would you rather work for your brother here on the family land? There's no hurry for you to decide. You have two more years before you're the age to start an apprenticeship.'

"At that moment I looked past my father and saw the pity in my brother's eyes. Not surprise, but pity. I turned away and ran down the hill, and then I just kept running. My brother followed, but this time I outpaced him until he finally gave up.

"I ran for miles until I found myself at the top of another hill, this one overlooking a level plain. I'd run northwest toward Sepphoris, and it looked like the Romans were setting up a military camp not far from that city. It made sense for them to keep an eye on Sepphoris, since my cousins who live there say everyone they know hates the Romans. Every time we'd go there to visit my uncle someone would start whispering about plots and rebellion. Their talk made my father very nervous, so we never stayed for very long.

"I lay in the hot sun on that hilltop all afternoon watching this army of faithless Gentile invaders lay out their straight lines and build fences around a big square of ground. As they were constructing a gate at the entrance I fell asleep.

"I walked home in darkness. No one said anything about missing me, so early the next day I left the house and went back to the same hilltop, and the following day, and the day after that. Now there were rows of identical tents inside the fence, all arranged in smaller squares. I can remember thinking that everything down there looked so well ordered, not like our home with grapes growing out of the dirt on their twisted vines, and with secrets and pity and a crooked, unknown path into the future.

"Then one afternoon something out of the ordinary happened. A man came out through the gate leading two animals, beautiful creatures like nothing I'd ever seen before. Well, Girl, you saw Bellator for the first time just two days ago so you know what I mean. While I was watching them, both animals lifted their heads and sniffed the air. Then the pair of them streaked toward my hiding-place like two arrows shot from a single bow. Before I could decide whether to stay put or get up and run they were standing over me, panting their hot breath into my face. I was terrified, but I got up on my knees and faced them, ready to meet my fate like Daniel in the lion's den.

"That's when I first met Claudius. He came strolling up behind the dogs and looked over their heads to see me kneeling there. He later told me, 'Your fists were clenched, your chin was thrust out, and your eyes were dry, so I decided to keep you.'

"Claudius said a word I didn't at the time understand, and the beasts sat down. Then he offered me a hand up and began my education. In that first Latin lesson he taught me the words for 'dog', 'boy', 'master', 'good', bad', and 'come'. Canis, puer, magister, bonus, malus, veni. In my first dog-handling lesson he taught me how to pet them and say canis bonus- 'good dog'. He showed me how to groom their coats with the stiff brush he always carried in his belt, and how to move my hand to make them sit. When those fierce creatures who were each double my weight followed my command I decided then and there what my apprenticeship would be, no matter what my family thought of Romans or dogs.

"That's how I came to work at the army camp and learn my trade, training and caring for dogs. Not a very practical skill in a land where dogs are distrusted and hated, but being around those beautiful, intelligent beasts suited my soul better than digging in the dirt to build up my brother's fortune. Every time I entered the camp through that Roman gate and saw the image of the she-wolf on the standard of the Sixth Legion, I felt like I was coming home.

"I've always had a way with animals, and year by year I worked my way up until I was Claudius' first assistant. Then about three years ago there was a pup born who wasn't able to suck his mother's milk. He was wasting away from hunger, so Claudius told me to take him to the creek and drown him. I asked if I could keep him instead, and all the other men laughed at me. But Claudius smiled and said, 'Go ahead, Jeremiah- take him. If the gods let him live, he's yours.'

"I carried the limp little body against my chest as I ran home to my one-room house on the edge of my father's property. I moved in there when I was 15 to shorten my walk to the camp, and, close to death as the pup was, that shorter distance may have saved his life. Once we got there I lit a fire to warm him. Then I held him firmly under my left arm and pried his mouth open with the same hand. When I looked inside I could see that his tongue was bound to the floor of his mouth, which explained why he couldn't suck. I took a sharp knife in the other hand, heated the blade, said a prayer for the Lord to guide my aim, and slit the little membrane under the puppy's tongue with the same wrist motion I'd seen during all my young cousins' circumcisions. The pup let out a short whine, and then he licked my hand. He licked my hand!

There was blood in his mouth, but his tongue was moving freely."

Now the story is about me, so I am happy. Even better, my Master reaches down to place his hand on my head, and I turn my neck so I can lick at his outstretched palm. I am a grown warrior, not a lap-dog, so he no longer pets or fondles me aside from a short pat of approval now and then. But for a moment both of us are back in that smoky hut and I am a scrawny pup ready for my first meal. At the touch of my tongue my Master gives a start like a man waking from a deep sleep. He takes back his hand, clears his throat twice, and returns to his story.

"My father had given me two goats, so right away I squeezed some milk directly into an old wineskin and fed my pup 'til his belly was dragging on the floor. In the morning I carried him to work with me in a cloth sling, and in a few days he was bigger than all his littermates. That's when Claudius said, 'Son, you ought to name him Bellator since he's already fought and won his own first war with death. He's a warrior who still has his milk-teeth!'

Soon my Bellator was trotting by my side on our two-mile walk to and from the camp each morning and each night. Later no matter how I hurried along he was able to run in circles around me. From the start we could all see he was the kind of dog that only comes along once in a lucky lifetime, but Claudius was true to his word. Even though this strong, beautiful animal would someday be worth his weight in treasure, Bellator was mine.

"And now he'll make my fortune for me. I own six of the pups he's sired, and all of them show a lot of promise. With the gold the king's paying me for Bellator I can start a new life in a place where dogs like these are valued, maybe even in Rome itself. This dog's Molossi bloodline and my training skills will give me a future to envy, and I will never be dependent on anyone but myself for the rest of my life. I will succeed without a denarius of any man's inheritance to support me."

I hear the triumph in my Master's voice, so I sit up, head held high. Even though Mary has still not told him about today's heroic act, my Master is proud of me. I am a warrior worth a treasure! But then Mary looks at me and my tail begins to thump against the ground, so all my dignity is betrayed.

Mary is not concerned with my dignity. She jumps up from the rock, puts both arms around me, and says, "So from the beginning God meant for this wonderful dog to live, and for you to have him. You guarded his life when he was a helpless puppy, and now he's guarding me. The world is so full of signs and wonders, isn't it, Jeremiah?"

This is the perfect time for my Master to hear about how well I guarded Mary this morning. Instead, he stands abruptly and says, "Come on, Boy. You must be as hungry as you were on that first day." He gives the sign to hunt, and as soon as Mary releases her hold on me I obey.

When I return from the meadow everyone is ready for sleep. Mary calls to me and I enter her tent. By the light of her little clay lamp I can see that she has already removed her outer garments and is wearing only the inner tunic she keeps on for sleeping. She is just laying aside her folded head-veil as carefully as a newly-promoted centurion lays down his plumed helmet. Mary smoothes the fabric with one hand and says, "It will be so wonderful to see Elizabeth again. My family always stayed with Elizabeth and Zechariah whenever we went to Jerusalem for Passover or for the Feast of Tabernacles, and she's always been so kind to me. In my earliest memory of my own life I'm sitting on her lap and she's brushing my hair and humming to me. There were no other children in the house so she could focus her whole attention on calming me down for sleep after all the excitement of the trip. There's such comfort and peace in this memory. On visit after visit I loved her lap so much that for years I hardly ever left it the whole time we were there. I used to trace the veins on the back of her hands with one finger. She told me they were rivers in a secret land, and she'd make up stories about the adventures the two of us would have there, stories full of bravery and faithfulness and kindness. Each tale ended with the two of us laughing as we came back home again."

Mary is moving her finger across the surface of the folded veil the same way she strokes the fur behind my ear, and just seeing it makes me shiver. She says, "The last time we were there, just three years ago, Elizabeth gave me this veil. She said, 'To me you'll always be the little girl who loved sitting on my lap, but at the same time I know you're also growing into a beautiful young woman. Soon it will be time to cover your hair and leave your childhood behind, but when you do

I want this to remind you that the blue sky over your head hasn't changed, just as our God hasn't changed. You can be a child and a woman at the same time, because you never have to forget all the wonder you felt in the beginning, when everything was new to you.'"

Mary lifts the veil and looks up as she holds it above her head like a canopy. "Look, Tobias," she says. "This is called linen. Elizabeth planted and reaped and spun the flax, and dyed it with the leaves of Isatis flowers she gathered in her old willow basket. I carry a piece of the sky, all woven tight with memories of care and love and adventure. She taught me to spin and weave, and she taught me patience. I know how long it must have taken her to make this, and I know how patiently heaven weaves everything together if we just wait long enough to see the patterns and color."

Slowly, carefully, Mary puts the veil away. She lies down on her mat and blows out her lamp, and once again I settle in by her side as she begins her evening prayers.

I do not know how to spin or weave, but I know blue. We dogs do not see all colors as humans do, but we can see blue. I know this because a visiting officer once came to Claudius and demanded color lessons for us. He said, "Romans wear red. These dogs need to know friend from foe, so from now on you're going to drill them on uniform recognition. I want you to make them run past men in red capes and attack men in brown capes. Have the men in the drill keep changing positions, as they would in battle." Of course in a real battle we know our own men by scent, not by inspecting their clothing. But an officer is an officer and orders are orders.

His plan did not work. No matter how many times the officer made us run this exercise we did not know how to do what he asked. He kept shouting, "The Romans are wearing red, you stupid mongrels! Red, red, red!" But all the capes looked the same to us, all of them the color of mud, so we just ran back and forth between the men. There was much barking.

Finally Claudius thought of trying different capes. Nothing worked until he ended up with what he called 'blue' instead of red. This time when he showed us what he wanted we could see that the new capes looked different, like the color of the sky. Soon we were running past the blue capes and attacking the men in the not-blue capes every time.

In the end the visiting officer yelled with spit flying from his mouth, "We're not changing the uniforms of the whole Roman Army for the sake of a pack of worthless curs!" Then he went away and Claudius gave us all some cheese.

I lay my head down for the night with the memory of that cheese still in my mouth.

DAY THREE

"Even though I walk through the darkest valley, I fear no evil; for you are with me... "

Psalm 23:4[v]

Chapter 13

It is not yet sunrise, but some light is just starting to filter through the cloth of our tent. Mary is already dressed, and when she opens the flap I follow her outside into the damp pre-dawn air. The camp around us is in slumber. Not even Ethan is awake yet.

She leads me to the field beside the road, but she does not give me any training commands. Instead I follow by her side, alert for any nighttime predators that may still be prowling. We are wandering in silence, not following any orderly path, when Mary stoops to gather something from the ground. It is a flower. I am sure Mary has seen flowers before, but she holds this one up before her eyes as if it is her first. Then she moves on with the single stem in her hand.

As the light grows we continue our slow irregular journey. She fixes her gaze on each flower for a long moment before placing it with the other blossoms in her hand. One by one she adds to the bunch until it is almost as big as my head.

Mary stands in stillness, face toward the rising sun, holding the fresh-picked flowers in front of her heart. Her eyes are closed, her only motion a slight movement of her lips. I stand beside her at attention, at one with the life flowing through us and around us.

Some time later we hear Ethan's voice: "Mary… Mary?" We move toward the caravan and see that Ethan is bent down and calling outside our tent-flap. He is surprised when we come up behind him. I am glad he is not the one tasked with guarding Mary, since it is so ridiculously easy to outflank him.

Mary pulls Ethan a small distance away from the wagon and shows him the flowers. She says, "These are for you to give to Rebekah. I saw a small bucket that will hold them very nicely hanging from one of your hooks inside. Don't you think some flowers will really brighten and freshen her gloomy little space? But they're not from me. They belong to you, for all the kindness you've shown me. See, I'm giving them to you. Now you can give them to her." Mary puts the flowers in Ethan's hand, turns him around, and gives him a little push. He turns his head back to say something, but Mary puts one finger to her lips and makes a "shhhh" sound. Then she points the same finger toward the wagon.

As he climbs toward the entrance, Mary reaches into our tent and starts rolling up the bedding. She says, "What do you think, Tobias? Scripture says, 'It is not good for the man to be alone.' Don't you think that's true for the woman, too? Loneliness turned inward is a terrible dark prison, with everything good in life locked outside. How will people ever understand God's love unless they have a spark of love in their own lives? Right, Boy?" I lick her face, and she laughs and says, "Right!"

Breakfast is another pot of delicious cracked wheat. Ethan is very quiet during the meal, and when we are finished he puts down his bowl and says, "Mary, let's trade chores. You wash up the dishes and I'll go get the Lady's plate." He must be very good at doing this because he comes back much sooner than Mary did yesterday. When he climbs down he brings Mary the Lady's things without a word and walks away to tend to his donkeys. Mary looks at me and shrugs. I am glad dogs are not as complicated as people.

The morning is bright and cool after the long rain, and the muddy road has had a chance to dry out overnight. We are making up for lost time and moving quickly when I catch a familiar combination of perfume, sweat and musk as a woman slips around the back of the wagon and into place at Mary's side. "Can I walk with you?" she says. "He'll leave me alone if I'm with you."

I want to warn Mary to stay away from this woman. Ones who smell like her are always causing trouble in the army camp. She has rancid colored creams smeared on her cheeks and lips and breasts, even on the tops of her feet. In addition there is burnt charcoal in stripes around her eyes and she peers out like a startled badger. The scented oil she has poured over her head cannot mask her dirty hair, and greasy curls hang down around her face outside the inadequate cover of her flimsy veil. Just having her nearby is offensive to me. But Mary smiles at her and says, "Of course- please join us. All are welcome here."

In addition to her unpleasant smells she also makes annoying noises. She jingles with every step because she is wearing beads strung on many small chains attached to her sandals and around her ankles and wrists and her neck and her waist, and she has brass things like tiny wind-chimes hanging from even smaller chains hooked through holes punched in her ears. Dogs do not like chains and I do not like her.

She says, "Everybody's talking about what your dog did to that camel-faced scum who tried to grab you yesterday. He's been pestering me for two days, telling me I have to come with him for free because he's the leader's bookkeeper. He even told two of my friends that if I didn't treat him right he'd have me thrown off the caravan in robbers' territory. So when he came pelting along stinking like an outhouse and yelling about being attacked by a lion that leapt on him from the hillside I laughed 'til my sides hurt. It got even better when the trader in the wagon behind yours came by during the midday break. He told everyone what really happened, and I got to laugh all over again."

Mary does not laugh with her. Instead she says, "I'm sorry he behaved so badly toward you. The threat of being thrown out into the wilderness all alone must have been terrifying."

The woman snaps, "I wasn't afraid. Don't you feel sorry for me- I can take care of myself." Her chin is held high and her face is pointed toward the road ahead of her. But then she turns her head to look at Mary, and there is a single tear falling from one of her eyes. She quickly wipes the back of a hand across her cheek. Now she has made a mess. The colored creams and charcoal are smeared together in a streak and one half of her face looks like it fell in a mud-puddle.

Mary reaches into her pocket and takes out a square of bleached cloth, but the woman waves it away. Instead she pulls a small polished metal mirror out of the pouch at her waist, and then reaches in again to fumble for a wadded-up cloth of her own. Without missing a step she rubs vigorously and wipes the smudged part of her face clean. Suddenly she is two people, one half a painted camp-follower and one half a young village girl like any other. As she walks along holding the mirror in her left hand, she fishes in her pouch with the right. One by one, she takes out little clay pots and recolors her face, ending with a stubby stick of charcoal for her eye. I still do not like her, but I do admire her coordination and discipline. Doing all of this while on the march was not an easy job.

When the woman is finished Mary reaches over and takes her hand. "My name is Mary, and this ferocious lion is called Tobias." She pats my head with her free hand to show that I am the ferocious lion. It is a joke.

The woman smiles, but she hesitates for a long moment before answering. Finally she says, "I am Levanah, It means 'the moon.' It's the name given to me in my new life. I've never told anyone what happened to me, but since we have time to kill and I'll never see you again, and since you weren't afraid to touch my hand, I'll tell it to you."

Chapter 14

The woman says, "When I was growing up on our little farm just outside Narbata, I used to look up at the stars every night and wish I could fly away from that place and come down somewhere nicer, better, more interesting. I always listened carefully in the synagogue when someone read the parts about faraway places, and when travelers came through town I used to follow them around and ask questions: 'Where have you been,' or 'What kinds of people have you met,' or 'What sights have you seen?' If I'd been a pretty little girl like my three younger sisters the strangers might have talked to me. Instead they just sent me off like a beggar, with no answer besides a cuff on the ear.

"My mother used to say, 'Why do you have to keep embarrassing your whole family? You'll never find anyone who wants to talk to you, let alone take you anywhere. Even more important, because of your annoying ways no one will ever pay a bride-price for you. With your bad manners and plain face we might well end up marrying you off to the old blind widower with his shepherd's hut out in the hills. That's the most of the world you're ever going to see. Would that be enough of a change of scenery for you?'

"Then when I was 14 I met someone. He came through town at harvest time with a crew of workers, and they camped not far from our home. He knocked at our door to ask if we'd sell him some eggs, and when he left he asked me to walk with him. Not one of my sisters, but me. As we strolled along he said to me, 'Those three back there are pretty enough, but I've traveled far and wide and I can tell you they're common looking. You, you're different. You're not like anyone else I've seen. I think you're exotic.' That's the word he used. 'Exotic'."

The woman gives a short little "huh", almost like a grunt. Her voice is harsh and she sounds angry, but I do not think her anger is for Mary. I decide she is not a threat.

"There's so much activity and commotion during a harvest that nobody missed us the times we slipped away from the fields. Besides, my mother always kept a sharp eye on my sisters; she never suspected that I might need watching, too."

There is another "huh," as if she is trying to growl but doesn't know how. I begin to find her interesting, like a puzzle with something hidden inside.

"Well, it turns out there's nothing 'exotic' about my story," she says.

Exotic is not a term used at the army camp so do not know what it means, but this time she spits out the word as if she has bitten down on something rotten. She takes a deep breath and continues.

"He left without me, of course. Then I found out I was pregnant, and when I couldn't hide it any longer my parents threw me out onto the road with the clothes I was wearing along with the cuts and bruises from a beating. My mother made a big show of it. She said, 'Everybody needs to see what we think of her. If they imagine we'd let our other girls act like that there'll be no husbands for any of them, no matter what they look like. Get rid of her and we'll all be better off.' So I guess the man in the bushes was right. I was different from my sisters, after all."

Mary is still holding the woman's hand, and now I can see by the movement of the muscles in her wrist that Mary is squeezing and relaxing her grip, again and again, almost like a heartbeat. After a short pause the woman continues to speak, but now she sounds as tired as a soldier in full retreat who has covered a long distance and still needs keep going.

"I walked all the way to the city of Caesarea and got there by nightfall. Before my father beat me he'd put two coins in my palm and closed my fingers over them so no one else could see. I went to the worst looking inn I could find and for my coins they gave me some supper and one night in a corner with a pile of straw for my bed. That meant I woke up the next morning with no family, no friends, no money, no food, and no place to stay.

The innkeeper pointed me to a doorway across the street, and the woman there took me in and gave me a job sweeping the floors and keeping the warren of small alcoves tidy after each use. It was… not a nice place. There was a steady stream of customers from the city and the Roman garrison, but the men weren't interested in me with my swollen belly. Still, no one beat me and I had a roof over my head and meals to keep me going.

"When my time came the woman delivered my baby, but she took it away before I saw it. She told me it was a boy, so somewhere in this world I guess I have a two-year-old son. Anyway, one morning a month after the birth she came to me while I was down on my knees scrubbing the floor and said, 'It's time for you to settle what you owe me for everything I've done for you. Have you got the money to pay up?' What could I say but 'No'? That's when she gave me a bath and some clothes and put me to work with the rest of her 'girls.'"

This is another word the woman spits out like spoiled meat. I know what a 'girl' is, but it must also have some other meaning to make her sound so disgusted.

"That's the day they changed my name. The woman who ran the place said, 'Your name is terrible. 'Esther'. You won't get far around here with a name like Esther. It smacks of religion, and religion is the last thing we want the men thinking about in this place, isn't it, girls?'

They all laughed, and one of them said, 'Even in broad daylight it's always useful to make them think of darkness and night-time, especially when they're with someone who looks like her. Let's call her Levanah for the moon.' So that's who I am and that's who I'll be for the rest of my life."

She drops Mary's hand and crosses her arms tightly across her midsection just under her breasts, which pushes the fullness of them up into the neck opening of her low-cut tunic. With defiance in her eyes she turns her head to look at Mary. She is daring Mary to do something, but I do not know what.

Mary does not say anything. Instead she places her palm on Levanah's shoulder, and I can see that Mary is moving her hand in circles, just as she does on my head. After a few moments Levanah's breathing slows and her tightly-folded arms relax a bit. When the woman's arms finally drop to her sides, Mary begins to speak.

Chapter 15

Mary says, "Esther, I'm so sorry. You can't be more than seventeen, not much older than I am, yet in the past three years so many people have already betrayed you. The man who came to your village, the innkeeper who sent you to that dangerous place, the woman who took your baby and then made you one of her 'girls', all the men who used you in that awful house, even the other women who laughed at you. But most of all, I'm so sorry your parents didn't support you and protect you. That must feel like the worst betrayal of all, since God himself entrusted them to care for you like a shepherd is supposed to care for his lambs."

The woman (Mary has decided we will call her Esther) is stumbling ahead with her head bowed and her eyes closed tight with nothing but Mary's hand on her shoulder to guide her. Suddenly her head comes up and, eyes still closed, she shrieks in a high voice, "Leave me alone, just leave me alone! I don't need your useless pity. You don't know anything. Compared to me you're just a stupid, ignorant child."

Mary's hand continues to stroke Esther's shoulder as if the woman had not just insulted her. After a few more moments Mary says, "This week I had to tell my own parents the same news. I have no husband, and I too am carrying a baby."

Esther's eyes fly open and she stops in her tracks so she can face Mary squarely. "You?" she whispers. "You're pregnant? And your parents threw you out and you got your hands on enough money to join this caravan? You're not very well-dressed, so you're not rich. Who did you steal it from?"

Mary takes the woman's hand again and the two resume walking, but now Esther leans her head toward Mary and looks at her with new respect in her eyes. I know this look because it is how the other dogs in the camp are when they see me, their leader. This is an important moment, when leadership is recognized.

Mary says, "You're right, Esther, my father isn't rich, but he himself brought me to the caravan, and he paid for my passage and gave me enough for my passage home again."

Esther is still speaking in a whisper. "Home again? You can go home again? Oh, I see. After nine months, right? Then you can go back without the baby as if nothing happened."

Mary says, "Actually I'm on my way to help my kinswoman Elizabeth. In just three months, when her own baby is born, I'll come back home. I don't know what will happen in my village when my pregnancy begins to show. I'm betrothed to a carpenter named Joseph, but he's not the father of this baby. I don't know what Joseph will do, or the neighbors, or the people at the synagogue. Joseph could publicly shame me and put me aside, and the law says the people in my town, the people I've known all my life, could even stone me to death. So there are a lot of things I don't know right now.

"But I do know these three things. First, my parents will care for me instead of throwing me into the street, so in this way my story is different from yours. That's not because I'm better than you are, Esther. It's because I have better parents.

Second, no matter what happens I am certain this child will always be a part of me, and I'm sure this is the same for you. I can't even imagine the pain you must have felt when your own son was taken from you. And the third part is also just the same for the two of us. We know from the psalms we both learned in childhood that the Lord is merciful and compassionate. Our God will never forsake anyone who cries out to Him in a time of suffering or need. And this third part is all anyone really needs to know."

I am waiting for Mary to get to the best part and talk about the angel and the baby becoming a king and the everlasting Throne of David, but nothing more is said. Hand in hand, the two walk on in silence. Esther's forehead is wrinkled with thought and her eyes are troubled, but Mary's face is calm. Mary places her free hand on my back, and the three of us move together through the late morning sunlight as if we have weathered our own private storm and emerged into clear skies.

Chapter 16

We stop for the mid-day break, and when Ethan climbs down Mary says, "Is it all right if my friend Esther shares our bread with us?" Ethan looks just as suspicious of the woman as he was of me when we first met, but he shrugs and says, "All right." I think Mary has become his leader, too.

No one says very much during the meal or the rest-time, but as Ethan is returning to his driver's seat Mary says, "Ethan, once we get started would you please sing the psalm about the shepherd for us? It would make such a beautiful prayer on this peaceful day."

Ethan looks at Esther with doubt in every wrinkle on his face, but as soon as the caravan is back on the road his voice rises up over the rumble of the wheels:

The Lord is my shepherd, I shall not want.
He makes me lie down in green pastures;
he leads me beside still waters;
he restores my soul.
He leads me in right paths
for his name's sake.
Even though I walk through the darkest valley
I fear no evil;
for you are with me;
your rod and your staff—
they comfort me.
You prepare a table before me
in the presence of my enemies;

you anoint my head with oil;
  my cup overflows.
Surely goodness and mercy shall follow me
  all the days of my life,
and I shall dwell in the house of the Lord
  my whole life long." [vi]

Ethan's final note fades into silence, and Esther's face is a mess again. There are two lines of black running all the way from her eyes to her chin, cutting a path through the thick greasy colored parts like Roman highways on a campaign map. Her nose is running, too, but this time she does not wipe anything away. Instead she says, "No, no, it's too late for me. Too much has happened, too many sins and nights and wrong turnings."

Mary has been holding her hand all the way through Ethan's song. Now Mary says, "Esther, there is absolutely no such thing as 'too late' with our God. From the dawn of creation until today is such a long, long time. Think of the promises God made to Abraham and Moses, promises that are just now coming true. Doesn't that tell you something about the Lord's patience? So please, Esther, please allow a little patience for yourself."

Mary is speaking like a leader, with confidence in her tone. Her words are not loud. Most humans do not know this, but real leaders do not need to shout.

"Oh Esther, Esther, from the day that stranger led you away from the harvest until today is such a small slice of time compared to all the years of your life. Your name means "hidden", and most of your days are still hidden from you like a flower's hidden, first in a seed and then in a bud. There can be wonderful surprises waiting for you, if you're just willing to look in the right places."

From the lines of her forehead I can tell that Esther is thinking very hard. This is the way my Master looks when he is trying to solve a training problem with a difficult dog.

Esther says, "Can it really be that easy? After all I've done?"

Mary answers, "If you choose to set your feet on a different path right now then goodness and mercy will follow you for endless days, just like the psalm says. You have so many years ahead to find the right path for yourself. You can go to a new village and offer to do honest work. There will always be people with kindness in their hearts who'll care about you instead of just using you. It won't be hard to find them. In time your own kindness will attract them to you. I promise you that all this can really happen, because nothing is impossible with God."

Esther is nodding her head in agreement. The wrinkles on her forehead have smoothed, and a small smile is forming on her face. Even with all the smeared and running colors she now looks like a girl close to Mary's age. My tail begins to wag in response to her expression.

Suddenly the driver of the wagon behind us calls out in a loud voice, "Hey, Levanah, don't forget about tonight! I've been thinking about your sweet body all day. I'm gonna squeeze you 'til you squeal, just like last night!"

Esther turns away from Mary and mumbles something. She drops Mary's hand and then clenches both of her fists. After a moment, in a deep and throaty voice she yells back over her shoulder to the man, "Yes, tonight. As soon as it's dark. I can hardly wait for it." Suddenly she is gone, darting ahead past our wagon, past Ethan's team of donkeys and off down the road.

Chapter 17

Now it is Mary who has tears on her face, but she is not a mess because she is not wearing charcoal and rancid creams. I nuzzle my head against her thigh to ease her sorrow, and she says, "Oh Tobias, the Lord puts troubled souls in our pathway for a reason. If I could just show her what God's mercy looks like, if I could point to it written across the sky or stamped on the outside of her skin like a birthmark. I know the shape of the Lord's compassion and the feel of it from the top of my head to the soles of my feet, but I just couldn't help her to see it or believe it was real. I think she heard an echo of it in Ethan's song, but one rude shout seemed to blot it all out in an instant. I need to trust that she's in God's hands just like the rest of us, and give the Lord time to work. And I can't very well talk to other people about patience and then let myself forget my own words, can I?"

I nuzzle Mary's thigh again. I think I know how she feels, because it is hard for me to understand Esther, too. Some people seem to be afraid that they are living in a place that is outside the goodness of creation. We animals never make this mistake. My Master and his rabbi friend once argued for a whole evening about what their writings meant in the beginning when God made everything and then said, "It is very good". They fought about what the word 'it' meant until I fell asleep.

Mary and I walk in silence, and I know that she is praying. I have noticed that sometimes even though she is walking forward she is in a state of stillness. At these times her breath is deeper and her eyes do not move from side to side to take in passing flocks of birds or patches of shade and brightness as the sunlight passes through the trees near the road. War-dogs are taught long lessons in concentration, but Mary would never need these lessons. When Mary is focused in this way as she prays I am attentive to the air around her just in case her angel might come near.

When we stop for the evening my Master comes for my training, and once again Mary joins us. Tonight our camp is not far from a river, and my Master brings me to a rocky area upstream from where the caravan people are calling out to each other as they bathe or wash their clothes.

He says, "Here we go, Bellator. Spring rains, deep water, a good current- time for some water drills." I love water drills! My Master wades in waist-deep, and we thrust and parry as I try to push him under the surface. When I am wet my fur is very heavy, and even an unusually strong man would find it impossible to lift me once I had him pinned. Of course I do not pin my Master long enough to drown him, and he is sputtering and laughing when we come out onto the shore.

Mary does not like this drill. I hear her cry out the first time she sees me push my Master underwater, and now that we are finished she is sitting on a rock facing away from us. My Master and I are both drenched, and as I shake myself at a safe distance he goes to Mary and sits in the fading sunlight on the other end of her rock.

She says, "All this work you do together is for war and killing. Tell me, Jeremiah, is that what he'll do when he belongs to King Herod?"

"That, along with hunting and acting as a bodyguard," my Master answers. "And as you know, he also makes an excellent companion. Since the king likes to copy Roman ways he'll probably want to have a chosen dog lie at his feet in front of his fire at the end of the day, and from what Herod's paying I can guarantee that Bellator will be his favorite. He'll be treated with great respect in war and in peace." There is pride in my Master's voice. "Not every dog is fit to do all of this, you know. Very few are as versatile as my Bellator. That's what makes him so valuable."

Mary says, "But who will King Herod be fighting? They say he's killed everyone in Jerusalem who disagreed with him, including his own wife and sons. His own wife and sons, Jeremiah!" Mary places one hand on her belly and I go to her side. I whine softly at her distress and she cradles my head on her knee even though my wet fur is soaking her garment.

Mary continues, "Is this the sort of thing he'll want a war-dog to help him with? What if Herod decides to wipe out all the people in the north and south who grumble against him, like your cousins in Sepphoris you told me about? The thought of what such a cruel man might use a dog like this for makes my soul cry out in pain."

I love Mary, but in this matter she must be mistaken. The man is called Herod the Great, and everyone knows that great kings are honorable and just. I wait for my Master to put an end to her discomfort by correcting her error, but instead he stands up and takes a step toward the water. He is facing away from us when he says, "There's no point in worrying about what other people might decide to do in the future. I can't control anyone but myself any more than I can control this river, and I certainly can't pretend to know anything about the behavior of kings. All I need to know is that I have a plan, and it's what's best for me."

My Master stoops to pick up a stone. He weighs it in his hand and then throws it into the river. Still looking away from us, he says, "But Bellator's a good dog, Girl. A good dog. I'm sure he can take care of himself."

With his hand pointing upstream, my Master gives me the signal to hunt, and when I return to him with my prey Mary is gone. My Master stabs his knife into my dead rabbits and slits them open with more force than usual. As he does this he says, "There's no reason to worry about you, Boy. You'll belong to a great king. You'll be just fine."

With this he walks off along the riverbank toward the sound of grimy travelers trying to finish washing up before the evening chill sets in. Army camp or caravan, humans are the same. They get dirty, they get clean, they get dirty again, but underneath nothing really changes.

By the time I finish my rabbits the riverbank is deserted, and when I return to the campsite Mary is already in our tent. She has left the flap open for me and I wriggle in beside her, happy to be inside out of the lonely night, happy to be home.

DAY FOUR

"The righteous are bold as a lion..."

Proverbs 28:1 [vii]

Chapter 18

Once again we are up before first light, and I follow Mary back to her rock by the river. She sits quietly with her face toward the water, but I am restless. Something is not right, and I begin to cast about with my nose to the ground. Just because I am a sight-hound does not mean I have lost the ability to do this, even though in this case it is difficult. At the start of the fourth watch last night I heard the drumming of rain on our tent canvas for a short time, and now the scents are watered-down and confusing. Because of this it is necessary to keep my nose very close to the stony soil.

My muzzle is directly above what I have been seeking when I first catch the concentration of rancid oil and something sickly sweet. I dig, and here it is: Esther's pouch of charcoal and color-pots, a tangle of her chains and beads, and two flasks that reek of her hair-oil and perfume. All of this is bundled together in the wadded-up cloth she once used to wipe her face. All the things inside the hole are soaked with fresh rainwater, which does not have the same scent as river-water. Even a sight-hound can tell the difference.

I do not bark, but suddenly Mary is beside me as if I had called her. "Oh Tobias," she whispers in the pre-dawn stillness, "where is she? Where's our Esther?" Mary runs to the river-bank and calls out, "Esther... Esther!" The only answer is the sound of water streaming over jagged rocks.

I launch myself out into the deepest part of the stream to retrieve something caught between two stones. The rushing water has twisted it into the shape of a thick rope, but when Mary unravels it we can both see that it is Esther's flimsy head-veil.

Mary holds the dripping fabric against her face, hugging it to her cheek the way a mother comforts a baby. Now Mary's face is wet and I do not know if it is from the scarf or if she is crying until I see her shoulders moving and hear her sobs.

"God sent her to me as surely as he sent me the angel. Esther was right there beside me, and the Lord was trusting me to reach over and help her, to say the right words or do the one right thing. And I failed her. I thought I had more time, another day or two, and now she's gone. I couldn't show her what a gift from God her life was, and now she's thrown it in the river like a sandal with a broken strap." I nudge her side with my wet head and she sighs, "Oh Tobias, I feel so helpless."

Mary reaches up over her head and pulls down the branch of a willow growing there beside the water. She ties the torn cloth among the leaves, and when she lets go it moves up into the rising pre-dawn breeze like a tattered battle pennant.

Mary stands beneath the willow with her face toward the beginning brightness in the sky. Her eyes are closed and for a long time her mouth is still, but as the light grows I can see that her lips are starting to move. It is difficult to hear above the sound of the river, so I lift my head nearer to her mouth. Softly, barely breaking her silence, she is singing.

"Even though I walk through the darkest valley, I fear no evil; for you are with me…"

As the light continues to brighten the surface of the river a flash of color catches my eye. On a flat rock that overhangs the water I notice a small blue bowl with the reflected sun glinting through its rim. It is made of glass, and its cover lies beside it. Glass is rare and fragile and does not belong on a rock beside a river. I am curious, so I move closer. I sniff inside and smell olive oil and ashes. I like olive oil, but this mixture is not something I want to taste.

When Mary opens her eyes I lead her to my discovery. She picks up the bowl and says, "This wasn't here when we left last night, and no one who owned such a beautiful thing would leave it here by accident." She rubs some of the contents between her fingers and says, "This is soap, Tobias, and it's half full. And look, there's no rainwater inside it at all. Someone must have taken off the cover after the showers passed by." Now Mary is nodding her head. "Esther," she says. "She washed herself clean. Whatever else happened, she washed herself clean in the river."

There is more light now, and I have learned the scent of Esther's soap. I do what I was trained to do when a comrade is missing so there can be a proper burial or even a rescue. I run the riverbank for the length of the caravan camp, but there is no sign of her on this side, dead or alive. I return to Mary and then plunge into the water and swim across the current. As soon as I reach the other side I sniff and know that Esther came out of the river in this same place. She must be a strong swimmer, which is unusual among the humans I have lived with, both Romans and my Master's people. Hardly any of them know how to swim. Most choose to drown instead of learning this useful skill. Esther did not choose to drown.

I am running now, up a narrow trail and over the crest of a small ridge. When I reach the other side of the hill I can see her not far ahead. She is walking like a country girl, dressed like every woman in every village. I do not know where she got her garment and veil, but they are clean and as I come nearer I can see that parts of them are still wet from her swim. I greet her with a bark. My tail is wagging, but she does not look happy and she does not reach out to me. "Go back," she says. "Please, please go back. I don't want to be found."

I sit at attention in front of her and wait. She stands rooted in place and we look at each other. Her arms are folded across her chest again, but this time she is not pushing her breasts up, and besides, the neck opening of this garment is much smaller than her old one.

At last she smiles and says, "Oh, you came from Mary, didn't you? Then that's all right." She does not touch me, but she does relax and unfold her arms. Her forehead wrinkles in her thinking expression. Then she says, "Here, I'll give you something to take back to my friend. She'll understand."

Esther bends down to some flowers growing by the side of the pathway, but the one she picks is just a stem. At the top there is nothing but a bulge folded up tight, nothing like the kind of blossoms Mary picked for Ethan to give to Rebekah. Still, when Esther places the stem in my mouth I take it with care. War-dogs are trained to carry messages. We do not ask what they mean.

By the time I get back to Mary's side of the river the sun is just coming up over the ridge, so my long shadow runs ahead of me and reaches her before I do. When it touches her she raises her head, and the dawn light makes the tears on her face glitter like Esther's glass beads. I cannot explain to Mary that Esther is over there on the path behind the hill with the full light already shining on her, but when Mary sees what I carry in my mouth her eyes grow wide. She leans down toward me for a moment, her gaze fixed on the stem. Suddenly she lifts her arms above her head and spins in a circle like a young girl dancing at a village wedding. She calls out, "It's a bud! It's a bud and she's alive! The Lord has sheltered her and kept her safe. And now she's on her way to wherever she herself chooses to go. And you, Tobias, you were God's messenger, you good dog. It's another sign."

Still dancing, Mary starts to sing again, but this time in a full voice: "'Give thanks to the Lord for he is good; his mercy endures forever!" She sings this three times before she stops whirling and grabs my head between her hands. She says,

"You are a beautiful, beautiful messenger, and this is a beautiful beginning for our day."

Mary takes Esther's flower bud from me, but even though I was careful the stem is crushed and limp from its swim across the river in my mouth. Mary pats my wet head and says, "Thank you, Tobias. I want to save this, and look how soft and pliable you've made it for me." Her fingers bend and twist the mangled stem and it becomes a little wreath like the bigger ones brides wear on their heads. It is just the right size to fit inside the blue bowl. After Mary closes the lid we move at long last toward Ethan and our breakfast.

Chapter 19

"Where's Levanah? I'm gonna beat you 'til you tell me where she's at, you scrawny old runt!" As soon as I hear the angry man yelling I run ahead of Mary. The driver from the wagon behind us has Ethan pinned against our front wheel. One of the man's hands is around Ethan's throat and the other is cocked back to strike. I am still on my approach when the man hears my battle-snarl and turns his head. I see the familiar look of terror come into his eyes, the fear that is the war-dog's greatest ally.

The man drops Ethan so he can fling up his forearms in a foolish attempt to protect his neck and face, but before I can lunge I hear Mary call out, "Tobias, sit!" This is not a command I have ever heard in the middle of attack training or combat, and it is difficult to obey. Instead of completing a graceful leap at the man's throat I find myself skidding toward him on my rump. I feel foolish, but am gratified to see that the man is still terrified. Even when sitting down I am a large fierce warrior with many sharp teeth. Perhaps he thinks my undignified arrival was some sort of a tactical maneuver.

Mary is by my side, out of breath from trying to keep up with me. "Good boy, Tobias," she pants. "Ethan is safe, and no one is harmed. Good dog!"

The man has uncovered his face and is staring at Mary's hand. He says, "That's her bowl! That's Levanah's bowl! Where are you hiding her at?" The man takes a step toward

Mary. He has forgotten his fear already, so I snarl again and he retreats.

. Mary says, "We just found this down beside the river. If you were her friend, you need to see what else was there. Come, and I'll show you."

"Friend!" the man snorts. "She's no friend of anyone's. I'm just taking her from one business owner to another. The woman she belongs to has an uncle who runs a house in Jerusalem, and he needs some younger girls. I've dragged her all the way from Caesarea. This here River Route's the long way 'round from there to Jerusalem, but that's the way I was going this trip, and I'm the only one the woman would trust with the job. That's on account of I'm one of her best customers, if you know what I mean. But I don't get paid 'til I deliver the goods, and now she's run off. The little thief is cheating me, that's what. And you're helping her to do it! I saw you yesterday, acting all friendly and nice to her, the two of you with your heads together so's you could hatch some plot to make a fool of me. And now you've got her hidden someplace. Well, all I know is somebody's gonna pay unless you show me where she's at."

This man is one of the truly stupid one who is ruled by his anger. Even though I am right here, his fists are clenched and he is leaning toward Mary again. I begin a growl, but Mary places her hand on my shoulder to calm me. "Come, and I'll show you where I found the bowl," she repeats, since the man was too stupid to understand her the first time.

Mary signals to Ethan to stay by the wagon. Then Mary and I lead the man to the river and she points to the flat rock. "The bowl was right there," she says.

"Why would she put it on a rock?" he asks. "She's always careful with that thing. It's her favorite trinket. And why would she bring it down here in the first place?" He is too stupid to ask what was kept in it. Instead of telling him about the soap, Mary shows the man the hole where Esther buried her things. The man reaches inside and paws through the items, even dumping Esther's pouch onto the ground and then peering into it as if he might find the woman folded up inside.

"Wait a minute," he says, now staring at the little pots scattered where he threw them, "these are her face-paints. How's she gonna make a living without them? Not with a face like hers!" The man laughs as if he has told a very funny joke. Then he repeats, "Not with a face like Levanah's," and laughs some more as he stomps on the clay pots and charcoal sticks, grinding them to bits under the heel of his sandal. "But," he says, abruptly serious, "she'd never leave these behind, not these or her fancy beads or that there bowl. They're all she's got."

A sudden wind moves through the willow branches and a corner of Esther's veil brushes across the man's forehead. He jumps back and looks all around before he notices the torn cloth waving above him. He snatches it out of the tree and holds it out to Mary. "How'd this get up there?" he demands.

"The dog found it out there in middle of the river jammed between those two rocks," Mary says. "I tied it to the willow in remembrance of her. Then I sang a psalm." The man stands by the water's edge while his brain calculates the distance to the mid-stream spot Mary has pointed out. It takes him quite a while.

While he is still thinking Mary says, "I called her name and the dog searched up and down this side of the riverbank, but there was no sign of her. Then he swam to the other side and brought back a flower bud. It was a message."

Suddenly the man bellows, "Shut up! Just shut up! I don't care what your filthy mongrel did. I've been cheated! She went and drownded herself and I've been cheated!"

He wads Esther's flimsy veil into a ball and tries to throw it to the ground with great force, but instead of falling straight down it drifts off like a swarm of gnats and settles itself on the surface of the water. The man's face darkens and he starts picking up stones and aiming at the floating veil, but none of them hit it. Now his forehead has large veins bulging out and his eyes become narrow slits. When men in battle look like this they do not fight with discipline. They usually make many mistakes, so I watch with interest to see what will happen. The man grabs a large rock and holds it over his head before hurling it down at the veil with all his strength.

The current whisks his target away just before his blow lands, and there is a great splash. The man stands soaking wet on the bank as the veil floats off downstream, free of his grasp.

Now the man starts to turn his furious face toward Mary, and this time she does not try to stifle my bare-toothed snarl. Even in his current enraged state he hears me, and as he quickly looks away from us he raises one hand to cover his throat. Stupid, stupid man, much too stupid to figure out the meaning of my swim to the other side and back. It was a waste of time for Mary to try to tell him something that is beyond him. It would be like explaining battle strategy to a sleeping donkey.

We leave him there as Mary and I once again move away from the river and back to Ethan and our breakfast. Mary must agree with what I was just thinking because she whispers, "That man refused to listen to the truth, didn't he, Boy? But we gave him all the facts. Levanah is gone, buried, washed away, and by God's grace he isn't looking for Esther at all. Her name means 'hidden', and God has hidden her from his sight as surely as the bud you brought back is hidden in this bowl."

Chapter 20

Ethan's hands are shaking as he serves our food, and I glance away. It is not polite to stare at a friend after his defeat in battle; it is best to let him lick his wounds in private. But as we finish eating Mary looks right at him and says, "Ethan, I can't imagine how frightening that must have been. Are you all right?"

He laughs with a raspy voice and says, "Oh, that wasn't much, Mary. There were fights and scrapes all the time back in my caravan days, and louts like that are just something you live with, like nasty weather or fleas. I may not be big, but I'm wiry. He wouldn't have done much damage before folks gathered to see if all the noise meant there was a good show going on. Soon enough they'd decide it wasn't a fair fight and shame him into stopping. No, the terrifying part was having to tell the Lady what all the shouting was about. She called me in and asked who Levanah was, and I wasn't sure what to say so I told her you'd explain it all later. I hope that was all right."

Mary says, "Of course. I'll talk to her when I bring in her breakfast."

Ethan thanks her, and while she's up in the wagon he gives me a big meaty knucklebone. My mouth waters at the scent of all that marrow, and Ethan says. "I was saving this for a stew, but you deserve it, Tobias. No matter what I said to Mary, as mad as that fool was I think maybe you just saved my life."

I am gnawing happily on my gift when Mary comes back, and she looks very happy, too. She says, "Well, Ethan, I told Rebekah that Levannah was a friend of mine who's left the caravan, but the Lady was much more concerned about you than anything else. I assured her that you were fine, and she told me to be sure we rubbed some oil on your throat to soothe the spot where the man grabbed you. Then she got up from her bed and found this for you. It was in a basket right below your flowers."

Mary is holding a small alabaster flask. When she removes the stopper there is a wonderful aroma, as if an entire cedar tree is growing inside that little bottle. Ethan says, "Oh, Mary, that's much too..." He stops speaking as Mary begins to massage some of the oil into his neck where the raw imprint of the angry man's hand can still be seen. Ethan says, "Ahhh", and there is silence.

This morning is turning out very well. Our breakfast is delicious, I have a bone full of marrow, Ethan smells like a beautiful tree, Mary has a message from her friend Esther, and the angry man is gone.

When it is time for the caravan to start out Ethan takes my bone and wraps it in a rag. "For later," he tells me. He is right; I cannot carry it in my mouth and be on guard at the same time. The angry man's wagon is now several places back so I will not need to snarl or bare my teeth at him as we go along, but there could be other threats.

. There is a different wagon behind us now, with a big laughing man and his wife sitting together on the driver's bench. As Ethan steers his donkeys onto the road the woman wiggles her fingers at Mary in a very friendly way, and Mary smiles and waves back. She is humming as we walk, and I recognize the melody that she sang earlier.

Dogs are very sensitive to music. Some of us even attempt to sing along with humans, but our tongues and throats are not shaped right to carry a tune so I do not try to join her, even though I remember the words. "Give thanks to the Lord for he is good; his mercy endures forever." Dogs do not know 'forever.' We only know 'now.' If I were created to sing words, this is what I would sing: "His mercy endures now." Since I cannot sing I dance instead, jumping up and bouncing on the ground, spinning in a circle three times, and Mary rewards me with a laugh. The morning sun is warm, the surface of the river glitters off to our left, there are smiling people driving the wagon behind us, Mary is humming again, and the scent of Ethan's anointed neck drifts back to us on a pleasant breeze. 'Now' is very good.

Chapter 21

As we slow down for our midday break I stiffen, fully alert as the annoying young man who tried to touch Mary approaches. He smells much better now. He has washed his robe and even the scent of old gravy is gone, replaced now with the dry smell of ashes. His hair and garment are covered with them. He looks older, partly from the gray color and partly because the ashes make his scraggly beard look fuller. His eyes are swollen and two lines run down through the ashes on his face, just like the lines Esther's tears made through her charcoal and face paint. The top of his outer tunic has a jagged rip in it, so his neck opening is big like Esther's old one, too.

As soon as he comes near I slip in front of Mary, but big as I am he does not seem to notice me. He says, "They're saying you were her friend. They're saying you were the last one who talked to Levanah before she… went into the river." The young man makes a choking sound on the last word. Now tears and snot start to run down his face, but he continues to speak. "Please, please tell me what she told you. They're all saying it was my fault, that she hated me, that she'd do anything to get away from me, even," the young man flings out his arm toward the river and his voice trails off.

Mary reaches across me to place her hand on the young man's wrist. She says, "You've rent your garment and covered your head with ashes. You're mourning for her." Then she is silent, but she looks at him with such tenderness that I want to bark a warning. "Remember what he tried to do to you", I want to shout, but I have no words.

The young man slumps to the ground and Mary seats herself in front of him, still touching his forearm. I lie down and crawl between them to remind Mary of what happened before.

After a while the young man says, "I have to mourn. I have no choice because I loved her. She was the most interesting person I ever met. She was always asking the other men to describe their travels, always coming up with the most wonderful questions so even those lunk-heads would remember details they didn't think they knew. What kinds of trees grow in Damascus? How tall are the buildings in Athens? Are the sands in Egypt the same color as the sand around here? And they'd answer her, all right, but soon enough out would come their coins and off she'd go with whichever one had the most."

The young man stiffens his spine and begins to pound his fist on the ground. I cannot see or smell anything there that he might be attacking, but I watch carefully in case something emerges from under the dirt. "If I just…had... some... money!" he yells, striking a blow with each word. "I would've given everything I had for a few minutes alone with her."

He has finished with his underground enemy, and he slumps down again. "I was too shy to talk to her with the others around. I just wanted her to come with me so we could talk by ourselves, so I could tell her about the things I've seen, so I could ask her to come with me and we'd travel the world together and she'd help me see things I would've missed without her. If only I'd been able to talk to her before it was too late."

I wait for Mary to tell him it is never too late, and I am puzzled when she does not give him this truth. But if my Master just handed me a rabbit I would not have the catching of the scent, the seeking, the chasing, the pouncing. So perhaps this truth is the young man's rabbit, and he will enjoy it more if he does all this for himself.

His voice drops to a whisper, and I lift my ears for better hearing. He says, "Then one day she started to hate me, just like that. I didn't know why, but one of the men said it was because I wasn't any good with women. He said I just needed experience. He told me you were traveling alone and that meant you were lonely and you wanted men to come and 'have fun' with you. Those were his words- 'have fun.' He said you could teach me the things Levanah was looking for. Well, you know what happened after that." The young man shudders and looks down at me lying there between them and I thump my tail, stirring up a small cloud of ashes. Yes, I know very well what happened after that, even if Mary did not tell anyone else about my victory that day.

The young man says, "After that she hated me even more. The sound of her laughing at me is the worst thing I ever heard in my life, even worse than the other boys in scribe school laughing when I couldn't get the words on the scrolls right. They mocked me every day when I stood up and struggled to read my assignments. I never teased them when they had trouble with their numbers, but that didn't seem to help. They laughed louder the day I was told to pack up my things because I wasn't ever going to be a scribe. Even the insults my father bellowed at me when I told him about my failure, even that didn't hurt as much as Levanah's scorn."

The young man sits up straighter and goes on, "But I was determined. I still hoped I could make her understand how I felt, even if it took a year, even if I had to follow her to Jerusalem and work as a laborer 'til I could afford to buy her time."

The young man's shoulders drop again. "Jerusalem," he says. "Now she'll never see Jerusalem or any of the other places she dreamed about."

Mary reaches into her pocket. She hands the young man her square of bleached cloth, and he blows his nose. When he is finished ruining Mary's nice clean cloth she says, "Tell me, did you ever threaten to have Levanah thrown out of the caravan?"

Even through all the smudged ashes and tears it is easy to see the shock on the young man's face. "Thrown out?" he cries. "Thrown out? Out into the wilderness? Out where there are robbers and wild animals? Our faith would never permit such a cruelty to anyone, let alone someone you love. No, I did not threaten her or anyone else with such a terrible thing."

Mary says, "If you never said that, then in truth Levanah never hated you. The ones who deserved her anger were the ones who told her that lie. But it was another lie told by one of those same 'friends' that sent you to me that day. They meant to humiliate you, cause trouble for Levanah, and bring harm to me as well. But God is good and now all their lies are washed away. And because you were brave enough to come here today, right into the den of Tobias my guardian lion," and here Mary pats my head, "you will now hear the truth."

As I remember things this miserable fellow who sits in front of her is not brave at all, but Mary must have her reasons for saying such a thing.

Chapter 22

"First," Mary says, "comes the truth about Levanah. She was a very young girl living with her family in her village when a grown man lied to her, used her, and then betrayed her. Next she was tricked into a debt she couldn't repay and forced to work for no pay in a terrible, violent house. She was treated like a slave for three years, a slave with no will of her own. She was on her way to a new 'owner' in Jerusalem when you met her. But now the hand of the Lord has erased Levanah from the face of the earth and set her free."

A low moan is building in the young man's chest as if he were a wolf about to throw back his head and howl, but he stops when Mary says, "My name is Mary."

Automatically he answers, "I am called Abraham." He is being polite. This is one of the things humans teach to their children when they are small. They have to use this form of greeting because they do not know how to sniff one another properly.

Speaking slowly now, Mary says, "And my friend's name is Esther."

Abraham looks around. He is confused, and asks, "Esther? Who's Esther?"

Mary answers, "Esther is my friend who was able to swim across the river early this morning."

For a moment Abraham continues to look baffled. After this he leaps to his feet and calls out, "Swim? Swim! She could swim! She's safe! Blest be the Lord, the God of Israel!"

Mary is smiling at him, but she says, "Sit down, please sit down. As good as this news is, it isn't something everyone in the caravan needs to hear about. I was the only one who knew, and now there are two of us." Clearly Mary has not thought about me or she would say, "There are three of us." I have four paws, so that is how many numbers I can count. Three is smaller than four.

Mary repeats, "Please sit down." Whenever Mary tells me to sit I obey immediately, but Abraham does not. Instead he walks around in small circles with his two hands on the top of his head as if he is trying to keep it from flying away like a barked-at crow. However, he has stopped yelling so Mary does not correct this disobedience.

When he finally seats himself he leans toward Mary and whispers, "This is a miracle to me. Every time I thought of the river closing over her head I couldn't breathe. I was a man walking around with a noose tightening around my neck, and now suddenly it's gone. Instead of seeing her under the water I can imagine her stepping onto dry land just like our people when they crossed the Red Sea. But why are you calling her 'Esther'?"

Mary says, "'Levanah' was only her slave name. It was given to her in her bondage, but it was never her own. That name was a weapon. They meant to embarrass her with it, remembering how Isaiah said 'the moon will be ashamed.' But it was never the truth. Her true name was always Esther, and now she has it back. The question is: now that you have the truth, what are you going to do about it?"

Abraham looks away toward the distant river and says, "I will carry her memory with me all the days of my life. That's more than enough for me."

Mary shakes her head and says, "But you said you loved her. You were mourning her like a family member, and now you know she's alive. Why don't you just go after her?"

Abraham folds his hands in his lap and looks at them as if they are an interesting puzzle he has never worked before. Finally he says, "She still hates me, you know."

"Well," Mary says, as if she is speaking to a small child who is not very smart, "why don't you find her and tell her the truth?"

"Oh, I couldn't do that," he answers. "I'd be afraid to try. She'd never believe me. Or there'd be other people around and I wouldn't be able to speak at all. Or by the time I found her she'd already have someone else who loved her, as beautiful as she is. She'd never pick me if she had another choice. Or maybe I wouldn't be able to find her at all. No, I'll just keep my memories and leave it at that."

At this moment Ethan arrives with bowls of hand-washing water and two plates with bread, cheese and olives. He also has a small wine-skin under his arm, and two wooden cups. He says, "I didn't want to interrupt you, but it's past time for you to eat something."

Mary tells Ethan and Abraham each other's name, and Ethan turns to leave. He did not have anything for me, and I wonder if he gave my share of the food to Abraham. Ethan takes two steps away from us and stops. When he turns around he reaches both his hands into the pouch at his waist, and then there on the ground in front of me he puts a big hunk of cheese and also my knucklebone. I sit at attention, but when he gives me the signal and says, "It's yours, Tobias", I am paralyzed. I love cheese and I love my bone, and I do not know which one to take first. When I hear them all laughing at me I lunge for the cheese and down it in one gulp. Then with the speed of a warrior I fall on the bone and there are sheds of dried meat and tantalizing marrow yielding to the satisfying crunch of my teeth. Mary pushes her washing water closer to me and everything is perfect.

I have licked both of their bowls dry and am still gnawing happily on my present when they finish their meal. Mary puts their dishes aside and says, "Abraham, hold out your hands." She does not say 'please.' She must truly be his leader now because he does what she said.

His open palms are facing upward, and she taps them one after the other as she says, "In this hand you hold love, and in this one you hold fear, the fear of all the things that might happen in the future. You are not like Tobias with his cheese and his bone. You can't have both. If you want to keep either your love or your fear, you have to throw the other one away. Please, please think carefully. At this moment you are being asked to choose."

Abraham sits and looks from one hand to the other as if he is waiting for something to pop up like a mole-rat. At last he says, "How can I know?"

Mary answers, "You can't. You can believe, you can trust, you can hope, but this isn't something you can know. Even if you try your hardest and do your best, even if you pray and you think you're following God's path for you, still things may not turn out the way you want. There is only one thing that you can know. If you let fear stop you before you start, then you'll end up with nothing."

Abraham lowers his open hands to rest on his knees. He closes his eyes. Mary moves into her stillness and I help her by dropping my bone between my front paws and laying down my head. The camp around us is quiet except for the sound of Ethan humming as he tends to his donkeys.

All of a sudden Abraham jumps to his feet and calls out, "Halleluiah!" One fist is punching the air above his head and he is laughing. "Halleluiah!" he repeats. "I've already lost everything, so I'm free! My place in the Temple, my father's approval, my home, my dignity, Levanah- all gone. I even lost a battle with a lion." Abraham brings a hand down on my head and gives me a playful pat. There is no fear in his touch.

"I have nothing left, but I'm still here," he says. "And Levanah may be gone, but Esther is still here somewhere, too, and she's lost everything, just like me. We're alive. That's the answer, and I have to find her so I can tell her. That's the gift straight from the hand of God. That's where the hope and trust and faith were all hidden, buried under all those other things I thought I needed."

At this moment Ethan comes to collect the dishes, and Abraham folds his arms around the little man in a hug that lifts him off his feet. Ethan stiffens all his muscles and turns a face filled with alarm toward Mary, but she laughs so he shrugs and relaxes. When Abraham puts him down Mary says, "Ethan, you've traveled this road so many times you must know every twist and turning of it by heart. Are there places near our route where a man can ford the river?"

Ethan takes several steps away from Abraham as he answers. "As a matter of fact we just passed one not long ago, back where the road took a sharp bend. There's a trail right there that leads off to the fording place. That's where someone's strung a strong chain across the water above a line of flat stones. I've never crossed it myself, but I've been told it isn't too dangerous, even now when the river's running high."

Abraham moves toward Ethan with his arms outstretched again, but Ethan grabs our plates and bowls and makes a quick retreat. Abraham calls out, "Thank you, friend!" to his receding back.

Mary goes into the wagon for the Lady's dishes, and after she brings them to Ethan she returns to us with the little blue bowl in her hand. She says, "After you cross the river you can make your way back to the spot opposite from where we camped last night. If you look straight across the water and see a willow tree growing on the bank on this side you'll be standing where Esther came out of the water. That's where Tobias picked up her scent." Mary smiles at me, and I can feel my ears rising up and cocking forward. I am very proud.

"Just follow the pathway you'll find there", Mary continues. "When you find Esther," tell her everything you told me. I think she'll listen to you if you show her this." Mary takes the lid from the glass bowl so Abraham can see the twisted-up stem and bud. Then she closes the top and places the bowl in his hands. Since Mary is his leader he does not ask any questions.

Mary completes her orders. "Do not wash your face or mend your garment before you find her. Your grief is proof of your care for her, and she has seen so little care in her life. And don't worry about what to say. The Lord will give you words, and if you can't manage to say them then look her in the eye and let your silence speak for you."

Abraham squares his shoulders like a proper soldier. He says, "Thank you. Just… thank you. Will you give me your blessing before I go?"

I have never seen a woman bless a man before. Abraham is very tall so Mary has to stretch to place her hands on his bowed head. She prays without speaking or moving her lips, but the joy on her face is a prayer all by itself. This must be how she looked in the presence of her angel.

Without being asked Ethan brings Abraham a stout walking-stick and a pouch that smells of bread and cheese, along with a wineskin. There are a few men in the army camp like Ethan, ones who stay in the background and notice what is needed. People do not usually pay any attention to them, but we dogs see everything. These are very good men.

When the caravan begins to move Abraham leaves us. His head is high, and the sunlight on the ashes in his hair make him look like he is wearing a helmet. And of course Mary was right. He looks very brave.

Chapter 23

Late afternoon shadows are beginning to lengthen. I am on watch, and my head sweeps from side to side as I scan our surroundings. Ever since Abraham left us Mary has been walking along deep inside her prayer. She would not notice it if we were surrounded by jugglers and tumbling acrobats so it is my job to be on high alert, especially now that the road is leading us past rough hills.

My vigilance is rewarded when I catch a flash of sun on metal at the top of the rocky slope just ahead of us. I am already halfway there when the band of robbers bursts over the crest and men start scrambling down toward the caravan. They did not expect to see a Roman war-dog charging them at full speed, and as soon as I open my jaws to bay they attempt to turn in their tracks and retreat. Pebbles fly as their feet slip and pivot, and all but one of them vanish as quickly as they appeared. In the blink of an eye only the frontrunner remains. He is sliding now, his feet carried down the hill by the treachery of the stony soil and his own momentum. There is a long knife in his hand and as I close on his advancing position I can smell his fear even before I see his beardless face.

I time my lunge to intersect with his downward path, and as I leap toward his throat the terror in his eyes seems to flash in front of me like a warning flag. Suddenly instead of an enemy I see a skinny, frightened boy, maybe even younger than Mary. In midair I adjust my attack and thrust my front feet forward. Now instead of my teeth hitting just below his jaw, my paws make contact with his narrow chest and we crash to the ground together. The shaking hand that holds the knife flails in my direction, and I close my mouth around his twig-thin wrist. But instead of snapping the hand off with one bite, my teeth stop short of the bone. There will be damage and scars to carry for the rest of his life, but that is all. I release my grip, and his eyes widen with both pain and relief.

I do not pursue him when he turns uphill and clambers away, crawling on his one uninjured hand and his knees. Instead I pick up the knife, which is now covered with his blood, and trot back to the caravan. My head is high as I carry my trophy down the hill.

Ethan's wagon is stopped at the bottom of the slope, and a crowd has gathered in front of it. Even the caravan leader is standing among them. All of them are watching me. This time there are many witnesses, and my story will certainly be told. I am prancing toward my admirers when my Master steps out in front of the others. I place the bloody knife at his feet, but when I look up I see the furrows of disappointment on his face.

He leans close to me before he speaks, his voice a whisper for my ear alone. "Where is the severed hand that held this weapon?" he asks. "Where is the body waiting to feed the carrion crows as a warning to other thieves? Did you forget that you're a Molossus? Have I left you too long in the company of a girl and an old man?"

My head drops below my shoulders with shame. My Master is calling me a coward. Even worse, he says being with Mary and Ethan is bad for me. But then he lifts the knife above his head and turns toward the crowd. "Look!" he cries. "The robbers are vanquished. My brave warrior has saved us all. Praise for Bellator! Praise for Bellator!"

Now the people are cheering and calling out my name, and the caravan leader is applauding loudly. Everyone is looking up at the gore-stained knife, but I lie down and try to flatten myself into the roadside dirt. Am I a hero or a shameful failure? For the first time in my life I do not understand my Master at all.

The caravan leader barks an order; "Everyone back to your places- we have miles to go before we make camp. And look sharp- there could be more scum like that bunch lying in wait up ahead. But we know how to deal with them, don't we?" He claps my Master on the shoulder, and the two men share a laugh as they walk away together.

When everyone is gone Mary comes to me and kneels by my side. My head is still down, but she bends over me and places her arm around the back of my neck. Her face is nuzzling my ruff so her breath ruffles my fur when she says, "Oh, Tobias, you were wonderful. Now I see what all your training is for. You didn't hesitate for a moment. Before anyone else knew there was a threat you were already racing toward the danger. You were as righteous and bold as the lion in Proverbs. God sent you to protect us and shield us from harm, and now we're safe. Even more important, I know you had the power to end that boy's life, but you spared him. This is one more sign that it was our merciful Lord who sent you into my life."

The tip of my tail begins to wag, and I lift up my head to rest under Mary's chin. I love Mary! But I love my Master, too, and the two of them are different people with different ways. My path has always been easy. I just follow my Master, and that is enough. But what would happen if he and Mary are not going in the same direction and both of them are calling me?

I do not like confusion. When my Master and his rabbi friend have their long arguments I just go to sleep. But now the disagreement is inside me, and I do not know what to do.

The caravan starts to move, and suddenly everything is the way it is supposed to be again. We jump to our feet, and it is my job to walk beside Mary and protect her. I am following my Master's orders, and Mary is resting her hand on my shoulder. All is well.

CHAPTER 24

Once we start forward the rhythm of paws on pathway soothes me. We walk, and the sun moves lower on the horizon, just like every other day. Then I hear footsteps behind us and the cheerful woman from the next wagon rushes up beside Mary. She is out of breath and laughing. "I just had to thank you for the way that wonderful dog of yours took care of those bandits back there. I feel so safe with our wagons so close and all." Even though she is smiling and calling me wonderful, I notice that she keeps her distance, and her eyes shift from Mary to me with a look of uncertainty. I wag my tail to reassure her, but my gesture sends her veering a bit farther away.

Mary answers, "Isn't the Lord our God good to us, sending such a brave guardian? We can give thanks together and praise the name of the Lord who holds us safe, body and soul."

The woman nods her head and is saying, "Blessed be the Lord" as she slows her steps and we leave her behind. She must return to her wagon because she has not trained properly for traveling any kind of a distance on foot. She would make a very poor soldier.

Before long her place by Mary's side is taken by a white-haired man with a long shaggy beard. In spite of leaning part of his weight on a walking staff, he still moves more easily than the short-of-breath woman did. He, too, calls me wonderful. The harsh words my Master spoke to me begin to fade like the pain of an injured paw after sufficient licking. Mary responds again with thanks to God for sending me. I am really starting to enjoy this afternoon.

For the rest of the day, one by one or in twos, men, women and children pass by us in a steady stream, each one hurrying to catch up with our pace or dropping back from their places ahead of us in the caravan, all of them straining to have a look at me.

I am pleased with their attention. Most of them call out to Mary, telling her how remarkable I am. How brave. How swift. How fierce in battle. I can feel myself prancing like I did before my Master scolded me. But like the cheerful woman and the old man with the staff, none of my admirers come near me. Even at a distance I am bothered by the fear that radiates from them more clearly than the sound of their words. Some of them start to ask how many men I have killed. One even wants to know how many times I have bitten Mary.

Long after I am tired of the lot of them Mary is still answering every comment as if it were the first. She gives her full attention to each one who speaks to her, even if she has already heard the same thing as many times as I have heard my Master's training commands. She explains again and again how thankful she is to the God who sent me to protect them all. The sound of her voice soothes me, so I listen to its rise and fall and ignore the words of the passing strangers. Usually when we walk she is deep in her silence, so this is a treat for me, a sound like music and better than a great hunk of Ethan's cheese.

When the small boy from the roadside approaches holding the hand of his Ama, my attention revives. He is still afraid, but he, too, whispers, "Thank you." This interests me. Mary is always thankful, but she fears nothing, just as her angel said. The child who was stalked by the wolves is now both truly fearful of me and truly grateful to me. Animals do not share this particular mixture of feelings. We can have both fear and respect, as the wolves had for me, but not fear and gratitude. We can pretend to be thankful to the one who controls our food, but we do not mean it. This child, along with the others who have approached us today, seem honest in both of their feelings People are complicated, and understanding them often seems impossible.

As the command to halt for the night passes along the caravan the travelers all return to their own positions since they all have tasks to perform. At last Mary and I are left alone, and when Ethan's wagon rolls to a stop she kneels down on the ground in front of me and places her two hands on my head. "Tobias, Tobias," she says, "don't ever let other people tell you who you are. Their mirrors are so cloudy and distorted, the images all twisted by their own fears and misunderstandings. Your one true reflection is in the eye of your Creator. Oh, Tobias, in the beginning God saw all that was and all that would ever come into being. That's when your own Creator said, 'It is very good.'" Her fingers are tickling the fur behind both of my ears, and everything fits together, her words and the dance of creation and the feel of her hands on my head. It is all very good, and I am once again balanced in my proper place.

Then a shrill little voice calls out, “You, Girl, let me see that dog!”

CHAPTER 25

There is a child standing behind the wagon. The setting sun flashes on the gold trim of her small sandal as she stamps her foot. "Now!, she shouts, and stamps her foot again. I have seen this one before, on the first day on the job when we met the caravan leader. She is the man's daughter, and she is nine years old.

Mary rises from the ground in one graceful motion. Facing the child, she says, "Hello. I am called Mary."

The girl says, "I didn't ask for your name, I said I want to see the dog."

Mary responds to this rudeness by smiling, stretching out her arm in my direction and saying, "Well, here he is. Behold!"

"I don't want to see him just standing around looking stupid," the girl snaps. "They say he ran with the speed of an eagle and attacked a whole band of robbers and left their bodies all torn to pieces and covered with blood. Everyone was teasing me because I missed it. So I want to see him attack something."

Mary turns in a circle and looks all around. She says, "Sorry, I don't see any bandits anywhere. Maybe later."

"Not later. Right now!", and the girl's foot stamps the ground again. She is not an interesting child. She is rude and repetitive. I yawn and lie down.

She walks over to me and pokes at my paw with her little sandal. She does not seem afraid, and I am tempted to snap at her tiny exposed toes to correct her behavior. But Mary is still smiling, so I lay my head down and ignore the irritating pup.

"If there aren't any bandits he'll have to attack something else. Tell him to kill one of those donkeys over there," she demands.

I raise my head from its resting place and focus on the child. I am not fond of donkeys, but I have a code of honor. Roman war dogs do not run wild and harm innocent non-combatants, especially not on the orders of small and annoying children. And besides, my friend Ethan loves these donkeys as if they were his own sons and daughters.

Mary's smile is gone now, and her face is troubled. "These donkeys are God's creatures, and they serve us well and faithfully. If anything happened to them their owner wouldn't be able to make a living, and he'd have to go hungry. .And besides, he really loves them, so it would make him very sad. Please think carefully. Do you truly mean to harm them?"

The child turns toward Mary and the small foot stamps down again, her heel so close to my mouth I can almost taste it. "You heard me, Girl", she shouts. "Command your dog to attack. How dare you question me! My father is the leader of this whole big caravan, and you're nothing but an old woman's servant!"

I send out a low warning growl, but Mary stops me with a look. She gets down on one knee in front of the child and bows her head. "What you say is true," Mary says. "I am a servant, a handmaid with no earthly power at all." Now Mary raises her head and looks up into the eyes of the child.

"I serve the Lady in the wagon, but there is a Lord all of us serve, you and I included, and His command is mercy and kindness. This is the command I follow, and I know this command is planted in your own heart, too, if you seek for it. This is my prayer for you, that you will find mercy and kindness hidden within you."

The child stands perfectly still, and Mary and I wait in silence. Suddenly the girl begins to make a sound like a screech-owl. She breaks and runs, and her wailed words fade as she dashes away. "I'm telling! I'm telling my father! You'll be sorry! You'll be so, so sorry."

Ethan comes back to see what all the noise is about, and since I have no words I nudge his leg with my snout to let him know I am not a ruthless killer and I would never harm his donkeys. He pats my head and goes to Mary, who is still looking in the direction of the screeching child. When she turns she is brushing tears from her face. "I'm afraid life is going to be very hard for that poor little girl," she says. "She has so many sharp edges to catch on whatever comes her way." Ethan looks puzzled, but instead of explaining Mary goes to Ethan's team and starts stroking the nearest donkey's back as she unbuckles its harness.

Ethan joins her, and I follow along. I have never been this close to the front end of these or any other donkeys. I am surprised when one of them lowers its muzzle and uses it to caress the back of my neck. The touch is gentle, and I stand still instead of leaping away. Ethan says, "That's right, Rosie, let him know he's one of the family." Soon all four of them are unharnessed and standing around me in a circle, their breath warming the air around my face. Instead of the imagined foul stench there is a scent of dried grass and honest sweat. I reach up and give Rosie's chin a tentative lick and she makes a low, unexpected sound like a purr.

They are looking down their long noses with great soft eyes full of curiosity, and I begin to understand why Ethan calls them his 'family.' Donkeys always appeared stupid to me when I was driving them along from the back, demanding that they go where I directed. It was Claudius who told me what these beasts were like, and I believed him without question. But now I can see not just intelligence but a kind of wisdom in their faces. All my former opinions about them are slipping away under the steady gaze of my four fellow-creatures.

Ethan squeezes in beside Rosie and puts his left arm around her and his right around the animal on his opposite side. "This lovely lady with the white face is Lily, and next to her is her twin, Myrtle. And that handsome sandy-colored fellow over there is Barley." I wonder if Barley is named for his color or his eating habits, which must be impressive judging from his rounded shape. Maybe I should invite him to trot along beside me tonight in my training session.

Ethan continues, "Of course everybody here already knows your name, Tobias, since Mary's always talking about you, although everyone else in the caravan seems to have you confused with that amazing Bellator fellow". Ethan laughs and I can hear Mary joining in from somewhere behind him, but I do not mind, even when Barley raises his head to bray along with them.

I hear the voice of my Master calling my name, and for the first time in my life I do not want to run to his side. Instead I walk, head down, unsure of every step. But when I reach him he is his old self, laughing and joking with Mary. "Cardamom!", he shouts. "That stuff costs a fortune. Who else but Ethan tosses it into a cook-pot at a camp fire? What a character!" He gives my head a friendly pat and says, "Everybody's still talking about you, Boy. My shoulder's been slapped so many times in the last few hours I feel like it went into battle all by itself. What a day!" My Master is in a very good mood.

All through our training my Master laughs and tells Mary stories about the people he talked with this afternoon. Sometimes he even forgets to give me a command when I return to him and I must sit and wait until he notices me, but this inattention is not meant as a punishment. He has never been famous before, and it makes him as excited as a pup on his first real hunt. My tail wags at his happiness.

Instead of counter-thrusting with her own tales of all those who visited us as we walked along, Mary listens to my Master and lets him have his joy without interrupting. She is giving him a gift, but he will never know about it or thank her. I do not think that being famous is Mary's joy. Just as she told me, she does not need other people to tell her who she is because she can see her reflection in the eye of God. This is why she hoped I would do the same.

Finally my Master says, "And here's the best part, Girl. Three of them are very rich men, and they asked if I have any other dogs like Bellator. I told them he was going to the king's palace but I was breeding from his bloodline, and they gave me their names and told me to contact them when the time is right. So today was a very good day for my plan."

By this time the last drill is finished and I am sitting by his side waiting for the command to hunt, but instead my Master turns to me and says, "No hunting tonight, Boy." So this is to be my punishment. I remain at attention, although I can feel my ears droop with disappointment. But my Master continues. "People have been giving me tidbits for you all afternoon, and there's more than enough good meat in my pouch back at the wagon for your supper." My ears rise and tilt forward. Mary would be disappointed if she knew how much of my joy comes in a wooden bowl.

CHAPTER 26

The aroma from Ethan's cooking reaches us as we approach the wagon. When we arrive, the caravan leader is standing by our campfire and looking over Ethan's shoulder as my friend stirs the supper. The caravan leader looks up, sees Mary, and takes a step toward her. Standing behind him is the small form of his daughter, who backs up into the shadows as we come near.

The caravan leader reaches his hand out to Mary and says, "Hello, my dear young Lady. I've brought you a visitor."

The child moves into the firelight and stands beside her father. She looks up at him, and when he nods she begins to speak.

"I have to say I'm sorry," she says. She looks up at her father again, and this time he smiles as he nods at her. She takes a big breath and starts again. "No, that's not it. I mean I want to say I'm sorry. I told my father what happened because I thought he'd say I was right and you were wrong. But… that's not what he said at all. I never talked to him about anything like this before. He's gone most of the year, so I don't see him very much. But my aunt Anna moved in to take care of me after Mama died, and Aunt Anna always says, "Never get familiar with the servants. Keep them in their place. You have a position to maintain.' She's always telling me, 'Some people are meant to give orders, and others are put on this earth to do what we say.' So that's what I thought my father would say, too.

"But I was wrong. He said everyone in the world has feelings just like I do. He helped me remember how I felt last summer when I stayed with my cousins and they were mean to me because I was little and they were big. And then he asked me if I really wanted to be a mean person who made someone else feel like that."

She is crying now, with the kind of inward barking sound children make when they try to weep and talk at the same time. "I didn't want to be a mean person. I just wanted to see what I missed, so the men in Father's wagons would stop teasing me. I just didn't think about how I might hurt the donkeys or you or anyone else.

"But my father, my Abba, he said that's how people get mean, when they stop thinking before they get past themselves. He says you have to keep thinking all the way to the end. So he helped me to think and now I'm so sorry." She does several little barks on the word 'so'. This amuses me, but no one laughs.

Mary opens her mouth to speak, but before she can say anything I hear a strange voice from above us issuing a clear command: "Come here, child."

We all look up and see a tiny slender woman standing in the opening of the wagon entrance. It must be the Lady, but I am unsure. I have never actually seen her or been close enough to pick up her scent, and this was not the yapping, whining voice I heard before. She does not move, but the light from the fire sparkles on jewels at her throat and wrists and on three of her fingers. The embroidery on her mantle and veil also catch the firelight as if someone has traced her outline in fine lines of silver and gold.

Before any of the humans can react she is climbing down, her foot planted on the wheel hub with the ease of long practice. By the time Ethan reaches her she is standing on the ground, straight as a legionnaire at inspection.

"Come here, child," she repeats, but this time the voice is soft, inviting. When they are standing together the woman is not much taller than the little girl. Jewels sparkle again as the woman holds out both her hands. "I am called Rebekah," she says.

The girl takes the offered hands in hers and answers with a polite bow, "I am Sarah, daughter of Josiah. My mother was named Naomi."

"Well, Sarah," the woman says, "we have a lot in common. I know what it feels like to be left behind by the death of someone you love, and I know what it feels like to be left out by others. And I too was told when I was very young that servants and workers didn't matter. But I never had someone as wise as your Abba to guide me when I was your age, so I never learned the lesson that was shown to you today.

"I never wanted to be a mean person, either. But no one ever taught me how to think things through past myself and all the way to the end. Just imagine all the pain and sorrow I spread throughout the years because I never knew something a nine-year-old could pick up in an afternoon! Do you know what a blessed and fortunate little girl you are to have such a wise and caring father, Sarah daughter of Josiah?"

"Oh, yes I do, Rebekah. My Abba even thought of bringing presents for the donkeys so they'll know I'm really sorry." The little girl releases Rebekah's hands, reaches into a cloth shoulder bag, and waves four unusually long carrots in the air above her head. The long floppy leaves flutter like a banner. All the humans laugh, but I take her action very seriously. Animals know that a gift of food is deeply connected with the life all creatures share in common. The donkeys will understand this. Josiah has made an excellent choice.

Ethan steps forward and takes Sarah by the hand, and as they move toward the donkeys I join them. This is an important ceremony, and I am their Guard of Honor. All four donkeys receive their carrots with dignity. They bow their heads to reach her outstretched hand, and Ethan shows the child how to pet their faces and scratch their ears in the way they like best. Then Barley brays for her and makes her giggle, and Ethan says, "Now it's time for us to eat, too."

When we get back from the donkeys everyone is sitting on small rugs on the ground around the fire, even Rebekah, who laughs and shakes her head when Ethan offers to get her a folding wooden stool. "Don't forget, Ethan, you're two whole years older than I am. You'd better save the stool for yourself," she teases, adding "but if you can manage to lower yourself to the ground I've saved a place for you right here next to me." The skin on Ethan's face becomes very dark, and although he ducks his head he cannot hide the smile that almost splits his face in two.

After the hand-washing Mary passes around plates of spicy stew, and Ethan brings out a platter of flatbread, almonds, olives and spiced dates. The caravan leader has brought a box of dried apricots and honey-cakes as well as two large wine-skins, so it is a real feast. My Master did not forget my bowl of tidbits, and he places it on the ground between Ethan and Mary. Then the three of them together give my signal and say, "It's yours!", and I am part of the feast, too. Even better than the bowl of meat, when everyone praises me for my bravery my Master joins right in. Perhaps he has forgotten to be ashamed of me.

Ethan says, "If today was dangerous, tomorrow could be worse. Right now we're camped outside of Jericho, and the road from here to Jerusalem is steep and treacherous, with bandits behind every rock. I'm glad our hero here is eating well tonight, since he may be very busy come morning."

My Master answers, "Well, my friend, as a military man I can tell you this. Rumors travel faster than caravans, and by now those scum that turned tail and ran from Bellator this afternoon have spread the word down the road to all the others. Of course, they won't say they were defeated by one dog." This is not correct since I did conquer them all by myself. But then my Master continues, "Why, Ethan, don't you know we're protected by a hundred armed guards, a troop of archers, and a whole pack of ferocious Molossi hidden in our wagons?" They all laugh, so now I know that this was a joke. Then the joke is over and everyone is looking at me and thanking me again for my protection. From dawn into darkness, this has been my favorite day.

After supper our three guests get up to go home and Mary leads me toward our tent. Only Ethan and Rebekah remain seated by the fire. As everyone is saying good-night my Master calls to Mary, "Tomorrow's your big day, Girl. I'll have you at your relatives' house before sunset!"

I know about my Master's plan, and I know I am going to King Herod's palace. And I also know that this is not where Mary is going. But tomorrow! I did not know anything about tomorrow. Tomorrow Mary is leaving me. Perhaps it is what Mary would call 'a blessing' that dogs do not know how to think things through to the end.

I feel an overpowering urge to turn my face to the sky and howl, but I am well-trained and disciplined so I force myself to clamp my jaws shut. Not even a whine escapes me. I do not want to trouble my friends, and it would frighten the donkeys. So instead I crawl into Mary's tent and lay my head down beside her for the last time. I feel her fingers move in the fur of my mane, and tomorrow goes away. If I were Ethan I would start to sing, but softly, so I would not wake her up: "Give thanks to the Lord for he is good. His mercy endures now."

DAY FIVE

"Praise the Lord from the earth... animals wild and tame"

Psalm 148:7,10[viii]

Chapter 27

Dogs dream, and our dreams are very real to us. I am alone on a mountainside, and deep snow covers all that I can see. The only dark spots are footprints on the crusty surface, and when I sniff the air there is a trace of Mary's scent. I try to follow her track, but the snow is up to the level of my eyes and I sink into it as if it is shifting sand. Ice coats my fur and weighs me down like a thousand pebbles attached to my skin. The footprints disappear and Mary's scent is fading. I become frantic, but the ice and snow hold me motionless. Then out of nowhere Mary's arm circles my neck and her sweet aroma fills me up like a wineskin just before it bursts. "Wake up, Tobias," I hear her say. I open my eyes and in front of my face I see the soft light of dawn filtering through the stripes of our tent. Mary is right beside me and there is no snow at all. I stretch to my full length and my front and back paws bump into the canvas end flaps. Mary laughs at me. All is well.

When Mary and I come back from what she calls our 'morning necessities' Rebekah is sitting by the cook-pot with a small wooden board on her lap. She is chopping apricots and almonds and as we approach I watch her hopefully, but her hands are so deft at the job that not a morsel falls to the ground. As we reach her she uses the side of the knife to slide her handiwork into the pot, and I sigh.

Mary says, "Good morning, and may God bless us this day."

Rebekah answers, "Blessed be the Lord indeed. Good morning, Mary. I was just praying for a chance to speak with you alone, and here you are!" Rebekah pats the ground by her side and Mary sits down next to her.

Rebekah looks different in the light of day. She is wearing a plain outer tunic and head covering made of fine supple linen, like Mary's blue veil only darker and not-blue. She has left her jewels behind, but even without the sparkling she is a woman who would draw attention. Her posture is excellent and she holds herself with a sense of command anyone in the Roman camp would recognize at once. I sit at attention, but when she speaks she does not issue any commands at all.

She says, "Mary, I need to tell you how sorry I am for the way I treated you." Rebekah takes Mary's hand and continues, "Yesterday was the most important day of my life. When I heard that child giving you orders with cruelty and contempt in her young voice, it was as if a bolt of lightning struck my soul and cracked me open."

Mary listens without speaking, but she places her other hand on Rebekah's knee as the older woman continues.

"Suddenly a searing light poured in and I saw myself at the age of 9, convinced my beautiful face made me better than everyone else in my village; and at age 14, married to the richest man I'd ever met; and at age 20, apple of my husband's eye for producing two healthy, smart male heirs; and at age 40, mistress of two magnificent houses with hundreds of servants and slaves, and still renowned for my beauty; and at age 60, at the height of my power and sure it would last forever because it had always been my right to have everything I wanted.

"Then my husband died and I overheard my two sons casting lots to see which of them would be stuck with me. I was filled with righteous anger and resentment until yesterday, when that lightening flash revealed a vision. I could see myself standing in layers and layers of deep mud topped with a puddle of self-pity, and I realized I'd created this mess all by myself. But the truly amazing part was this. All I had to do to step out of the morass was to look around me in the clear, wonderful light and see it for what it was. Suddenly I was able to laugh at myself. That's all it took, after all these years. One good laugh and I was free.

"So I got up and got dressed in my finest things so I could come outside for supper and offer a proper apology to you, and, even more, to Ethan. I was just putting on my jewelry when Sarah returned with her very wise father, and I heard her offer her own apology."

Mary is smiling, and I wonder if she is thinking that the bright flash of light means Rebekah was visited by an angel, too. Then a wrinkle forms on Mary's brow. She says,

"Rebekah, I'm so happy for you. But how did you know what Sarah said to me? Weren't you in your bed all yesterday afternoon?"

Rebekah lifts Mary's hand and gives it a friendly squeeze. She says, "Actually, Mary, there's a small knothole in the side of the wagon, right where I lay my head. I'm able to hear everything anyone says as long as they're close by."

Mary's face becomes pale, and Rebekah says, "Yes, dear child, I did hear what you confided to Tobias that first day. It made me feel even sorrier for myself, if that was possible. Now not only did I have a worthless servant who couldn't ride inside the wagon and take care of me because she was too busy throwing up. On top of that she also talked to dogs and saw angels.'

Rebekah pauses and pats Mary's hand. "Please don't look so concerned, Mary. From now on your secret is locked in my heart, and before this I never spoke of it to anyone. Who could I have told? Certainly not Ethan. I thought if I frightened him at the beginning of the journey maybe he'd turn back and I'd have to return to Benjamin's house. Before I left I heard my daughter-in-law planning a party to celebrate my departure. She was crowing, 'Now that stuck-up wife of dear brother Jacob can be the one who has to listen to the old witch whining night and day.' So going back to Benjamin wasn't a possibility.

"In my misery I thought you were a lunatic and Ethan was a coward. That's how self-pity twists everything around so it can feed on itself. Now I can see clearly, so I know that you walk in the company of our kind and merciful God every day of your life, and Ethan is as brave as… well, as brave as Tobias here."

For the first time Rebekah reaches out and touches my ear. I wag my tail, she laughs out loud, and now we are friends, too.

Ethan returns from his donkeys, we share a quick breakfast, and we are on the road again for the final day of our journey.

Chapter 28

The day is clear and cloudless. Mary is beside me with her hand resting on my mane. Rebekah is sitting up on the driver's bench next to Ethan, and he is laughing and singing snatches of songs as we go along. From time to time Rebekah's voice joins in with what Mary calls harmony. This 'harmony' is something the soldiers sometimes do when they sing while they are marching, and I swing my tail with the music.

The road begins to rise when we reach the hills my Master talked about last night, and the donkeys have to pull harder and harder to move the heavy wagon. Ethan sings them a song about donkeys dancing in the moonlight, and when he hits an especially high note Rosie starts to bray, followed by Barley, until all four of them fill the air with their noise. The humans are all laughing so hard we nearly miss hearing the command to halt that comes down from the front of the caravan.

I have been scanning the hills for danger ever since we reached them, but I do not know why we stopped. Nothing out of place on the rocky slopes has alerted my eyes or my nose, and it is much too early for our midday break. We hear a distant shout that becomes louder and clearer as a message is passed from person to person along the line of the caravan: "Rockslide ahead, road is blocked, stay in place." Ethan calls the words out to the people in the next wagon just as my Master jogs up beside us. He is not smiling and there is a single crease running across his forehead, so he must be busy solving a difficult problem.

"Bellator, patrol!," he commands, and he points to the team and wagon to show me my perimeter. "Ethan, stay here and be on alert. Keep Rebekah and Mary in the wagon. Josiah says rockslides are natural enough during the spring rainy season, but we're forced to sit here like roosting hens 'til it's cleared. I'm picking out some strong men to go forward and work on it, but it might be hours. Keep the team in harness; we have to be able to maneuver if we're attacked." My Master hits the side of the wagon with his palm as he rushes past us. "Take care," he says, and he is gone.

We have our orders. Immediately Ethan jumps down to make room for Mary on the driver's seat, and I begin my one-wagon-four-donkeys patrol. One by one my Master's emergency recruits move past us toward the rockslide, some running, some grumbling, some stumbling along with their frightened eyes scanning the hills. The stupid one who hated Levanah lumbers past us with his head down and eyes on the ground. He looks submissive, but I growl anyway, and he hastens his pace.

I do not question my Master's orders. Staying near Mary and guarding her should make me very happy, but I am also disappointed that my Master did not choose to use my many skills to help with the rockslide. Perhaps he is forgetting all my hours of obstacle training, when I practice climbing over, digging through, and swimming across many difficult barriers. Sometimes we dogs are put through these exercises with a paw bound as if we are lame, sometimes with a sled of heavy rocks harnessed behind us, sometimes with a sack the weight of a grown man strapped to our backs. No matter what the test, I am always able to keep moving forward longer and farther than any other dog.

I would like to be up in front helping to dig through the rockslide, or demonstrating my strength by pulling a rope tied to a stubborn block of stone. It seems instead that today my own way of moving forward is to walk over and over in a small square pattern around Mary and the wagon. There will be no glory today, or admiration for what I am doing. I will need to find my satisfaction in the act of being faithful.

I sense a familiar vibration beneath my paws, the pounding of many hooves followed by the friendly scent of sweating horses. A commanding voice shouts in Latin. "Make way! Make way for Rome!" Ethan grabs the donkeys' harness and leads his them to the left against the rocky hillside just in time as a troop of cavalry overtakes us from the rear. The soldiers ride by single-file in perfect order, the crests of their helmets rising up into the bright morning sun. I feel my heart beating in rhythm with the hoofbeats, all my instincts and training pulling at me to join them, to follow, to once more be a part of their great and glorious empire. But I have been given my orders, so I remain by Ethan's cumbersome wagon and his donkeys, patrolling this small space, torn between my call to faithfulness and my longings for action and renown.

As the final rider passes by he turns his head and looks at me. I wonder what he sees: a hardened war-dog standing at attention, or an ordinary house-pet? I myself am not sure which one I am. Until I am a part of King Herod's forces, I am caught between these two answers. This feels like the time I tried to make a running turn on a polished marble floor. I cannot find my usual firm footing.

After the echoes of the troop's passage have faded, a strange procession approaches. Josiah is pulling two foolish looking donkeys along by their halters. One of the animals is piled with many layers of blue cloth until he looks like an enormous sea turtle with hairy legs and a long gray face. The other donkey might be a giant porcupine bristling with sharp metal quills. They are a sorry sight compared to the controlled power of the Roman horses.

"Catch!," the caravan leader shouts, and he throws something from the turtle-donkey at Ethan. Ethan unfolds a blue military cape and holds it out at arm's length.

"Put it on, friend," Josiah orders with a laugh. "Last night we joked about all the bandits imagining we had a hundred armed guards, and now we do! I remembered one of our merchants was carrying an order of new swords and capes for King Herod's personal soldiers, so I did a little borrowing. Keep everything clean and shiny and no one at the palace will ever know." Josiah removes one of the porcupine donkey's quills and says, "Here, just carry this sword where it shows; we don't have any scabbards."

Ethan tries without success to look fierce and war-like in spite of his size and the awkward way he holds his weapon. Compared to the Roman cavalry troop he is an embarrassment, but from a distance and to untrained rabble I suppose he will be fearsome enough. Mary and Rebekah clap their hands and then Ethan completely spoils the effect by tucking the sword under his arm and gently petting both the turtle and porcupine donkeys on their noses. Josiah shakes his head and moves on.

I try to find some of my lost valor in a pleasant morning of routine patrol. I do want to protect Mary and Rebekah, and I am very good at guard duty. I have always enjoyed the rhythm of it, and this time it gives me another chance to show my skills to Mary.

Ethan, however, has no such skills to demonstrate. I am sad to report that he will never be a soldier. He spends half his time fussing with the donkeys and the other half fidgeting with the place where the wool cape rubs against his neck. He does not smile once until we see the rock-clearing crew moving back to their places as the "Road is clear, prepare to move!" shout is passed along. Mary hops down, Ethan climbs up, and we are back to normal, although almost a full morning has been lost.

The grade of the road continues to rise, which is difficult for the donkeys and the people who are walking although it is nothing to me, especially now that Mary is back by my side. She whispers to me, "The capes and swords were on this particular caravan for a reason, right, Tobias? It's another sign. God is watching over us, and He can even use King Herod's army to protect us."

She has spent her morning visiting with Rebekah, and now Mary is silent again. I am proud that in her silence her breathing is soft and regular despite the difficult terrain of our march. Like me, my Mary is strong and in excellent condition.

We have not covered much distance when the midday halt is called, but we have left the area of the rockslide far behind. This shows good tactical planning, and I wonder if it was my Master's decision. Our rest time is short, just long enough to water the animals, eat something, rest the tired muscles of the rock-clearing crew, and return the capes and swords to the merchant.

When Josiah comes with his two donkeys to collect King Herod's borrowed things there is a short heavy-set man at his heels. The man never stops complaining as he inspects and folds each garment and wipes each blade with a soft square of leather. Merchants who come to the Roman camp are just the same. Sometimes the quartermaster brings one or two of us dogs along when he meets with anyone who wants to sell him something or make a delivery. We are there to make the merchants nervous so they will go away faster. It is unfortunate that Josiah did not know this trick.

At the end of our break my Master and Josiah meet at our wagon. At first I think this is because Ethan has the best food on the caravan, since right away they sit on the ground and Mary brings them plates overflowing with good things. They only drop one plump olive, but Mary whisks it away instead of letting me have it. She only does this so she can split it with her fingernails and remove the pit before she lets me eat the tiny snack from her hand This is much better than licking it off the dirt.

My Master calls to Ethan, "Time for our meeting, my friend," so they are not just here for food.

Ethan brings me some oil-soaked bread when he comes to sit beside them, and while I am eating it Josiah says, "We've lost four hours, even with this shortened break. No chance of reaching Jerusalem by nightfall. Ethan, you have the most experience on this route. When the light fades do we push ahead in the dark or make camp one last time?"

Ethan stops to consider this, and the other two wait for his response. Finally he says, "The road will be wide and clear at the point where we lose the light, but the real problems come up when we arrive outside the city. They probably won't leave your usual large camping space at the caravansary empty that late, so the caravan would have to split up and try to locate individual places in the dark. Everyone will be exhausted, tempers will flare, and there might even be violence. I vote to camp on the road tonight and get a fresh start in the morning."

Josiah nods and turns to my Master, who says, "Ethan's right. And besides, there's no moon tonight. Trying to protect the whole length of a caravan traveling in the pitch dark when you can't tell friend from foe would be very dangerous. We'd be much safer in one place." Any Centurion would approve of my Master's reasoning.

"Good. We're all in agreement," Josiah says. "Camp as usual tonight, Jerusalem in the morning. Let's get going." Ethan is collecting the plates as Josiah stands and strides toward his place at the front of the caravan. If they let dogs vote, I would happily agree. All tactics aside, Jerusalem in the morning means another night in the tent with Mary.

Chapter 29

"Tomorrow, for at least one moment, everything will become as clear as day, Tobias." Mary is whispering in my ear as I lie in the darkness by her side. "As soon as I see Elizabeth, I'll know one thing I can hold on to." She hugs my neck as she goes on. "My angel was real. I have no doubt about that. But God is so great and I am so small. The ways of God are so far beyond anything I can imagine, and yet in these past few days I've found a space deep within my soul that's bigger than the earth and sky, all warm and filled with light, and there's a peace that turns everything I see, everything I experience, into one endless sign of God's love. I am very sure that I was meant to make this journey, but what happens next is part of that endless sign, and anything, anything God wants to do in me is what I long for."

Mary sighs. She is holding me so tightly that my body moves with the rise and fall of her breath, and for a moment what she has been saying fits with how animals live inside creation, where everything belongs in its own way, nothing is lost, and every move of each creature is a part of the whole dance. I do not understand endless, but if love is what Mary calls this dance, then we are dancing, she and I, as she sighs again.

DAY SIX

"Lord, my heart is not proud..."

Psalm 131:1[ix]

Chapter 30

I hear my Master's voice outside the tent, but he is not speaking to me. "Girl? Wake up, Girl. It's time to go," he says. Last night he told us we would leave the caravan before first light. We are going to bring Mary to Elizabeth before my Master and I keep our appointment with the king's Master of the Hunt. My Master said leaving the caravan to the other guards would be safe because no robbers would dare attack this close to Jerusalem. This is because everyone knows that when Herod's soldiers hunt down a suspected criminal they are allowed to make sport of their prisoner until the man begs to die.

I can only make out the whites of Mary's eyes as she opens them in the darkness, but then she smiles and her whole face emerges from the moonless night that surrounds us. "Thank you, Jeremiah," she calls. "I'm all packed and ready."

"Tobias, this is an important day for both of us," she says. "Let's go, Boy!" She lets me out of the tent and my Master is waiting. He is carrying his staff and his full pack is on his back. In just a few moments Mary comes out dressed in her garment and veil and carrying her sack of belongings. The three of us are well prepared for our journey.

Last night Mary said goodbye to Ethan and insisted he did not have to get up before dawn, but as we turn to start down the dark road I hear him whisper from the front end of the wagon, "Wait, you can't leave without something to eat!"

There is a spark from a flint, a flame flares, and we can see Ethan with Rebekah at his side. Ethan has a horn lantern in one hand and a cloth bag in the other, and there are tantalizing smells of yeast and almonds and spices. I also catch a strong scent of cheese. The sides of the bag are bulging, and I can feel my mouth watering at the sight. This promises to be much better than the dried rations my Master carries in his pack.

Rebekah is carrying a wineskin in a sling made of narrow woven strips that gleam like silver in the lamplight. She hands the wineskin to my Master, telling him, "For you, our good friend." Then she reaches to her shoulder and unfastens a gold pin shaped like a flower, which she places in Mary's hand.

Rebekah draws Mary into an embrace and says, "I hope this lily will remind you of the flowers you gathered for Ethan to bring to me. It was the first freely-given gift anyone had given me in many lonely years. I will never forget you, and all your kindness and courage. You brought love into our lives, and you, my child, will walk in the love of God all the days of your life. In the meantime, we'll see you again in three months' time. Ethan insists on coming back to escort you home to your parents, and I'm coming with him."

Mary says, "Oh, Rebekah, the pin is beautiful. Thank you. And it will be wonderful to have both of you with me when I go home. You are so good to me."

Rebekah places her hands on Mary's head in blessing. Then the woman whispers in Mary's ear, "And may you and your holy child bless us in return."

Ethan gets down on one knee in front of me. He places the lantern on the ground and then he caresses both of my ears. "Take care of yourself in Herod's palace, old friend," he says. I think we are both surprised when tears spring from his eyes as he says, "Please… take care."

Next he goes to Mary, but he does not speak. Instead he picks up her sack of belongings and his hands do something to the long carry-rope, Now it has two loops and her shapeless bag has become a back-pack, which he fits onto her shoulders. Mary puts her arms around him and gives him her best gift, which is silence.

Then Ethan and my Master slap each other on the shoulders, and Ethan places something in my Master's hand. Through the cloth wrapping I can smell both cheese and my knucklebone. I will miss Ethan very much.

As we take our leave our two friends are standing side by side. When Ethan lifts the lantern to cast more light on our path I can see that Rebekah's head is resting on his shoulder. Mary must see this too, because she gives my head an energetic pat and says, "Yes!"

On our way to the front of the caravan we pass Ethan's tethered donkeys. I move among them and one by one we touch noses in farewell. Then Barley nudges my side and sends me on my way.

Chapter 31

We move along the road past the still-sleeping caravan. Once we leave the lantern-light behind, the shapes of wagons and tethered pack-animals form blocks only slightly darker than the surrounding night. As we move along, gray light starts to filter into the sky to reveal the moving figures of two of my Master's guards, who call out in muted tones as we walk by, "All is well, sir."

Just as we clear the front of the camp a small figure breaks from the shadows and darts toward us, but I recognize the scent so I am not alarmed. Sarah flings herself at Mary and throws her arms around her waist. "Mary!", she pants. "Abba said if I woke up before sunrise I could come out here all by myself and say goodbye to you, so I did, I woke up all by myself! And I brought a present for Tobias!"

I smell flowers and crushed stems, and the child places something around my neck. Mary says, "Oh Sarah, thank you for waking up so early just to see us, and thanks even more for making such a thoughtful gift."

The child hugs Mary and says, "When I'm a grown-up I want to be just like you. I told Abba about this last night and he said I should say it to you in person and out loud. That makes it an official promise, so I'll be sure to remember it forever."

Mary returns the hug and they kiss each other good-bye. I knew from the start that Josiah was standing by the roadside keeping watch, and now he raises his hand in a parting salute. My Master returns the gesture, and we proceed down the empty road.

Usually it would be dangerous for such a small party to travel alone, but I am not worried. My Master has his staff and his long knife, I have my teeth and my impressive size, and Mary has her angel. I am confident we will be safe, although I am uneasy about how fearsome I may look with a collar of flowers draped around my neck.

It is a great pleasure to walk between Mary and my Master, with their matched easy stride and agreeable manner. Long marches with soldiers who dislike each other can be so unsettling that sometimes I find myself wishing for an ambush just to break the tension.

The sky is now streaked with the coming dawn, and one by one the birds on the surrounding hillsides begin their songs. This usually means breakfast is not far away, so it is my favorite time of day. Both Mary and my Master turn their heads to the east when the first sliver of the sun breaks over the horizon, and without a word or signal we all come to a halt.

Mary speaks, and her voice joins with the rising notes of the birds:

"The mighty one, God the Lord,
speaks and summons the earth
from the rising of the sun to its setting.
Out of Zion, the perfection of beauty,
God shines forth."x

After a quiet moment my Master adds, "Amen, Amen."

And now it is time for breakfast!

Chapter 32

We only pause long enough for Mary to wrap rounds of flatbread around some cheese and spiced dates, and for my Master to pour hand-washing water from his old leather flask. They eat their food as they walk along, and Mary does not forget to give me small hunks of Ethan's delicious cheese as we go. When the cheese is gone we pause again and the two of them drink some water. Then my Master pours some water into Mary's cupped hands, and she offers me the sweetest drink I have even known.

The sun is partway up the sky when the road curves around a hill and my Master stops and points ahead. Mary says, "Jerusalem! Zion itself, in all its beauty!" Their eyes are higher up than mine so I cannot actually see the city, but I can look at Mary's face and imagine how wonderful the sight must be.

We move aside to make room for some civilian horsemen galloping up from behind us, and before long we are surrounded by foot traffic and carts and wagons pouring in and out of the city, as well as countless pack-donkeys and merchants bound for market. My Master slips the leash over my head, but when he tries to remove Sarah's flowers Mary says, "Please, Jeremiah? That's such a happy memory for me." My Master shrugs and the wreath remains, and even though I know I must look foolish I don't mind at all. My Master must agree that I do not have the appearance of a proper war-dog because he hands the leash to Mary.

My Master turns onto a smaller roadway where there is not as much commotion. He says, "We'll move much faster if we skirt around the city. This will get you to your kinswoman's much sooner." I do not want Mary to get there sooner, but it is my duty to obey him.

Mary walks beside me with her fingers stroking my mane. I want this moment to go on and on, but in spite of my wishes the sun continues to move across the sky. Suddenly Mary's hand loses contact with me as she points ahead. "There's Zechariah's favorite wine-seller. And look, that's the home of a little girl I used to play with on our visits here. I'll have to ask Elizabeth what my old friend Ruth is doing now." Mary puts her hand back on my neck and I can feel the excitement coursing through her fingertips. Even though she is still by my side, she is already leaving me.

We are moving past a high terraced hillside when Mary says, "This road curves around and climbs the hill to pass by Zechariah's front door, but there are steps up ahead on the left that lead right to Elizabeth's back garden. Let's go look for them!" She rushes ahead, pulling me along and leaving my Master to follow, which is not the proper order at all. Everything is moving too fast. I am not ready for this, but her enthusiasm draws me forward in spite of myself.

We come to a stop at a large flat rock beside the road. Part of the stone's bulk is set into the bottom of the hillside. Other similar stones rise up above it in an irregular line. It does not look safe to me.

My Master catches up with us and says, "Girl, I promised your father I'd deliver you to Zechariah's door. What will I tell him if I let you break your neck before you get there?" My Master sounds irritated. He has just run along a public street chasing a girl and a large dog with a ridiculous wreath around its neck. And besides, I agree with him. The long way around will give me more time, and I need more time or I will start to howl and embarrass him even more.

Something moves high above us. A woman carrying a large basket is coming out of the house at the top of the hillside. She walks forward between the narrow cypress trees that flank the door. The woman turns and sits with her back to us on the low stone wall at the edge of her terrace. Mary looks up at her and whispers, "Elizabeth." There is such raw longing in her voice that I no longer want to hold her back.

My Master says, "Is that your kinswoman?"

Mary answers, "Yes! Yes, she's right there, just at the right moment. We never told her I was coming, but there she is, as if she were waiting for me."

I am a dog, but even I can tell that this is another sign. So the stone steps will be safe, and if they are not then her angel will carry her up the hill. My Master nods, and I wait for her to leap up the hillside "like a deer in the mountain places".

Instead, Mary goes to my Master and places her hands on his shoulders. "Thank you, Jeremiah," she says. "You've been a guardian and a friend and an answer sent from heaven. Without you this journey could never have begun, and I'm so grateful. Wherever life takes you, you will always be in my prayers."

My Master smiles a smile I have never seen on him before, like the look on the face of a child with a lap full of squirming puppies. Then he bows his head and kisses her forehead.

Now Mary's arms are around my neck and she is burying her face in my mane. "Oh, Tobias," she says, "my beautiful, beautiful friend sent by the God of all creation to stay by my side and keep me safe. Go in peace, Tobias. Go in God's peace."

She kisses my forehead, and her encircling arms crush the wreath against my neck. The aroma of the flowers blends with her scent and she is gone, moving up the rough stones as if she is dancing on a polished marble staircase.

As soon as Mary reaches the garden the woman stands up and turns to greet her. I am a sight-hound, so even at this distance I can see the billowing front of Elizabeth's garment. Both women lower their gaze as Mary places a hand on the curve of the older woman's stomach. Just as Mary said, this is the moment when everything becomes clear. Our journey was made for this, and Mary has her answer. Her story will now go on, but I am no longer a part of it.

Elizabeth steps back and lifts her hands high in the clear morning sun. Her voice cries out, but it is not with distress.

Mary is speaking now, and a breeze carries snatches of sound down to us. She is not singing, but her voice has the cadence and joy of a song. Only a few words are clear. Soul…holy… mercy ... promises... forever. These are all Mary-words. I do not understand their meanings, but I will keep these words to remind me of my time with her.

My Master rubs his hands together and says, "All right, Bellator, she's safe with her relatives. Our job is done. Come on, Boy. We have a very important appointment in the city."

The leash tugs my head around, and I can no longer see the top of the hill. My Master pulls the flower-wreath off over my head. My neck ruff must be tangled with the stems because I feel bits of hair tearing out. It does not hurt, but I whine anyway, hoping to let some of my sadness escape. "Sorry, Boy," my Master says. He tosses the wreath on the ground next to the road and I see it lying there as we pass by, wilted flowers twined with brown tufts of fur. I do not howl. Instead I follow my Master toward Jerusalem.

Chapter 33

It is not far to the city gate, only a few miles, and as we near the entrance my Master stops to shorten my leash. "Ready, Bellator?", he asks. "All right, Boy, time to make me proud."

We pass through the portal and pivot to the right. Immediately the sheer sides of three separate palace guard-towers loom over us. The high wall of the palace grounds lies straight ahead, and with so many stone surfaces my Master's footsteps echo as if an entire troop is marching through. The two of us walk at parade attention, erect and formal in our movements just in case someone has heard us enter and is watching from above.

The appointment was set for the sixth hour of whatever day we arrive, so the sun is directly overhead. This is when the King's Master of the Hunt always enters the courtyard in front of the palace as he returns from exercising his dogs. My Master knows this because it is written on the small scroll he carries in his pouch. My price and the name of the king's man are there, too. Sometimes at night my Master reads it to me.

We come to a halt in the paved space surrounded by the towers and the high palace wall. The massive fortifications cast no shadows at this hour, so we wait in the hot sun. No one else is here. Apparently King Herod's doorstep is not a place where townspeople people choose to gather.

The whole place is motionless except for my Master's hand, which flexes and relaxes its grip on my leash. He is tense, but I am not. There is no match for me in this whole country. I am the pack leader of the Roman She-Wolf Legion's war-dogs. My Master knows this, but he has told me many times that his whole plan depends on what happens in this final test. He is not a trained and hardened warrior, so he worries.

Hooves clatter on the pavement from the direction of the city gate, and the strong scent of agitated dogs reaches me. We see three mounted men wearing blue capes like the one Ethan borrowed, and each man is leading four unruly dogs. The hungry-looking animals snap and snarl at each other, making their leashes strain and twist. They wear collars of thick leather studded with long iron spikes, and their heads lunge from side to side with undisguised aggression. Some have fresh slashes on their flanks or sides; others have scars.

The horses are reined to a stop in front of us. Two of the men ply their whips in the air and the dogs crouch at the sound. The man in the center speaks, but he does not greet my Master. Instead he says, "Ah, good, my Molossus, my latest acquisition. Time to try him out and see how he gets along with his new friends."

These dogs are not my friends, so maybe this is a joke. The other two men laugh, but the sound is grating and without humor.

With a wave of the hand toward my Master the leader commands, "You! Don't stand there like a doorpost. Go ahead, turn him loose!"

Dogs live in the now, but in this moment I can see my future. Even though this is the palace of a king, it is a place without discipline or honor. These ruined animals are not the enemy, but I will need to kill one or more of them in the next few moments, and even that will not be enough. I will be goaded into violence at every turn at the whim of these men or others like them. I will fight and kill for no reason. I will forget my training and my Master, and even worse I will forget Mary. All this passes in front of me in an instant as I feel the leash slipping off over my head.

I take one step toward the unruly pack before I stop. Suddenly I roll over on my back. All four of my paws flail in the air as I expose my belly to the snarling curs on their taunt leashes. I whimper. I whine. I allow a warm stream of urine to leak onto the hot pavement, and its strong odor envelops me. Then I hear the men guffaw, and one of them bellows, "Look, he's got two pretty flowers tucked in under his pretty chin! Here, kitty kitty!"

The other man asks the leader, "Do we let the pack have him?"

The leader curls his lip and answers, "No! If they kill him I'll have to pay the price I signed my name to, and the king'll have my guts on a plate of onions. Ride on." They are still jeering and hooting and making cat noises as they turn their horses and drag the snarling dogs through the inner palace gate.

Now it is quiet in the courtyard. My Master looks down at me. He reaches out and pulls two dried blossoms from the fur under my jowls. The petals flutter to the ground as he crushes them between his fingers. I roll over and stand in front of him. I am ready to face his wrath or his bitter disappointment, but I am not prepared for what happens next.

My Master begins to laugh. He throws his head back and makes snorting sounds. He bends at the waist and supports his hands on his knees while his shoulders shake. Then he throws his arms around his belly and makes a noise like all four of Ethan's donkeys put together. High above I can see sentries looking down at us over the tower walls, and even when one of them shouts a challenge my Master does not stop. I nudge his leg and herd him out of the city gate, and still he laughs.

Out on the road he puts the leash back around my neck. He is still chuckling when we come to a small well by the wayside. We both take a long drink and then he sloshes a bucket of water over my rump. I shake myself and drench his legs and sandals, which sets off more laughter.

Now I smell better and the noonday sun will soon have me dry. My Master is not angry even though his feet are wet and I have ruined his plan. He is walking with his hand resting on my head for the first time in my life, and no dogs have died.

We travel back by the same route that led us to Jerusalem until my Master leads me into the shade of a roadside olive tree. He sits down on a large rock. He has been as quiet as my Mary for the last mile, and now as he begins to speak I watch his face carefully. I have never seen this expression before. His muscles are relaxed, and he is looking directly at me, not past me as he focuses on his next task.

"Well, Bellator,' he says, "I guess I need another plan."

He does not sound distressed or ashamed of me or sad, and he is no longer laughing, so I am confused. For the first time in my long memory I lift up a forepaw and place it on my Master's knee. He looks down at my paw and sighs. He says, "I didn't know what to do back there. As soon as I saw the spikes on those collars I knew I couldn't leave you in that place, but what choice did I have? I didn't want to touch the money from such a demon's bargain, but I couldn't just say I'd changed my mind. The man had a contract with my name signed at the bottom, as well as an army at his back. I didn't see any way out other than taking a stand beside you and going down together in a desperate, hopeless fight."

Finally my Master smiles, and I can see how he is feeling. "But you saved us, Boy. You saved us both. I know you weren't really afraid, but..." He pulls my head into his lap and grabs me around my ruff, almost as if we are wrestling. "You did it, you brave, smart warrior! You out-maneuvered the lot of them right there in their own stronghold, even though our enemies were within shouting distance of a whole garrison and you were outnumbered 12 to 1 by those poor starving curs.

My Master is proud of me. This is very surprising. He is still hugging my neck and now he is rocking my head from side to side on his lap. He continues, "And the best part? Those flowers stuck in your fur! At first when you rolled on your back all three men were in a rage, but when they saw the flowers it turned the whole thing into a big joke. That meant they could ride away laughing. They had a good story to tell, and that's worth a lot of mileage in a company of bored soldiers. Getting bits of that idiotic wreath stuck on you was a real piece of luck."

I cannot explain to my Master about Mary's signs, so I wag my tail instead. He gives my neck one last squeeze and says, "Come on, Bellator. I need to get to Josiah at the caravan camp and collect my pay. I may never have enough money to move to Rome, but I'll bet word will get around about how you handled those bandits back on the road. I think I'll be able to breed and train your Molossi pups and make a decent living in Galilee."

There is a plan, and we are back on the road. Once again my Master places his hand on my head and we move forward in silence. A flock of birds wheels overhead, and I notice that his eyes do not follow their passage or the shadows they cast on the pathway. I think he has changed more than just his plan.

JOURNEY'S END

"For he will command his angels concerning you
to guard you in all your ways.
On their hands they will bear you up,
so that you will not dash your foot against a stone."

Psalm 91: 11-12[xi]

Chapter 34

When the road curves past the flat stones that lead to Elizabeth's garden we look up, and there high above us against the blue of the sky is a small streak of lighter blue. It is Mary's veil. She and the older woman are sitting together facing away from us on the low wall. My Mary. I was never going to see her again, and here she is! I cannot help myself. I bark with joy, and there is no correcting "hsst" from my Master.

Mary jumps to her feet and whirls around toward us. She waves both arms in the air and then her hands come together over her head. When I hear the distant sharp sound of her clapping I bark again.

My Master kneels beside me and whispers into my ear. "You're a good dog, Tobias. A very good dog." He tickles me behind both ears as he slips off my leash.

My Master stands up at attention and the leash falls to the ground. He faces me and raises a formal Roman salute, holding himself as still as a statue of Caesar himself. I have never seen anyone salute a dog before and I do not know the protocol, but I sit up straight with great respect in my bearing, and my eyes return his steady gaze. After a long moment he pivots to the hillside, cups his hands around his mouth and shouts, "Mary, he's yours! He's all yours."

Mary moves her arm in the sign for 'come' and I bound up onto the first stone step. When I pause to look back at Jeremiah he salutes me again and then turns the salute into the gesture for "go". He is smiling and nodding his head as I turn to continue my ascent.

At every upward leap I can see Mary's face more clearly. The climb is long and steep, but it seems to take no effort at all. I do not see anything shimmering in the bright sunlight, but I think Mary's angel might be helping me.

Watch for Book II, *Mary's Dog: Bethlehem*
For more information go to http://www.MarysDog.com

DISCUSSION/REFLECTIONS QUESTIONS

(For free printable sets of these and other versions including one for teens, go to **http://www.MarysDog.com**)

What was Mary of Nazareth really like?

The Bible gives us hints and clues, but much is left unwritten. My hope is that by raising questions each one of us can reach a deeper understanding. The goal isn't for us to end up with identical conclusions. All of these questions are designed to be open-ended. The responses are meant to be personal, not right or wrong. (The story is narrated by a dog. This should make it crystal-clear that this is a work of imagination, not a claim of black-and-white fact.)

My hope is that If we can "walk a mile in her sandals" and see Mary's familiar story with fresh eyes, we may find a new personal connection to God's love and the gift of life we all share. Sometimes this kind of connection happens when we agree with what we read. But sometimes it's when we say, "No, that's not it," and we start digging into what bothers us about it. Either way, as long as we are respectful of one another we can all grow "in wisdom and in grace."

This guide can be used for personal reflection or for a 4-session book group. There is an added section at **http://www.MarysDog.com** for an optional 6-session group.

Week 1- Chap. 1-9 (Forward, Preface, and Day One)

(Someone please bring a small snack to share.)

In a moment of silence, let us be open to guidance and grace...... Amen

1. Even though most people in her society shy away from dogs, Mary reaches out right away and pets the animal. Does this tell you anything about the way the author sees her? Does this image ring true for you, or do you see her with different qualities? How does this relate to our relationship with the rest of creation?

2. In this book Mary's parents have trouble accepting the reality of her angel and his message. How did you relate to their response? Would you have written her parents' reactions differently? How would you yourself react if a teen in your family wanted to go off on a long trip all alone after a similar claim?

3. Mary interprets her sickness in the swaying wagon as a sign from God about the truth of the angel's message. Does it seem to you that God speaks to people through such everyday signs, or just through major events, or maybe not at all? Can you recall any such "signs" in your own life?

4. Mary asks Ethan about his life and then listens carefully to his story. Have you ever had anyone in your own life who would listen to you with this kind of patience? Have you ever been able to offer this gift to someone else?

End with a prayer for the lonely, and thanksgiving for all we've been given.

BONUS ACTION: EATING LIKE MARY

Share a snack in silence and slowly savor the flavors and textures. Give it plenty of time, and then share your responses.

Week 2: Chapters 10-17 (Day 2 and Day 3)

In a moment of silence, let us be open to guidance and grace...... Amen

1. When the young man tries to grab Mary, Tobias pushes him away. Were you surprised at the idea of Mary being threatened by violence? The young man misinterpreted the fact that Mary was walking alone. Afterward, when Mary is silent, Tobias wonders is she might be praying for the young man. What is your response?

2. Mary is not afraid to reach out and touch Levanah, even though she is clearly "impure" by the standards of their religion. Would you have written this differently? Would you yourself honestly want to walk next to Levanah?

3. As Levanah tells her story, do your feelings for her change in any way? Does it make sense to you that Mary shares the secret of her own pregnancy with this stranger? What do you think of both Mary and this "woman of the world" being teenagers?

4. After Levanah leaves, Mary feels that she's failed her. She trusts God, but she's afraid she didn't do enough on her own part. Does it ring true to you that Mary would feel this way? Do you yourself ever feel this way?

End with a prayer for people who are outcasts, and thanksgiving for all we've been given.

BONUS ACTION: SEEING LIKE MARY

During the next week, take at least one walk or spend time at a window and truly see what's in front of you: a cloud, a leaf, a squirrel, something specific. Allow yourself to just gaze, with no words or practical thoughts.

Week 3: Chapters 18-26 (Day 4)

In a moment of silence, let us be open to guidance and grace...... Amen

1. Levanah believes what Mary told her, so she transforms herself into Esther and begins a new life. What immediate changes do you see in her? Do you think this kind of change is possible in the real world? Is there any way we can support someone who's trying to make such a change?

2. The young man who tried to grab Mary returns, but now he reveals himself in a different way. Does that seem realistic to you? Have you ever struggled to explain yourself to someone? Has anyone in your life tried to get you to change your view of them?

3. Mary tells Abraham he has to choose between his love and his fear, because he can't have both. Do you agree with her? How do we experience love versus fear in our own lives, or in our world?

4. Tobias launches himself at the robber but decides in mid-air to injure rather than kill him. Can you trace any steps, large or small, that led him to this decision? His Master and Mary have different responses to this action. Have you ever had two people you cared about react to you in conflicting ways?

End with a prayer for those who live in fear, and thanksgiving for all we've been given.

BONUS ACTION: Think of someone you don't approve of and try to see that person through eyes of compassion.

Week 4: Chap/ 27-34 (Days 5, 6, and Journey's End)

In a moment of silence, let us be open to guidance and grace...... Amen

1. Rebekah (the Lady) finally shares her story and ends by telling Mary that that "one good laugh" was all she needed to free herself from her self-pity and resentment. Does this ring true to you? Does laughter have anything to do with how you see your own self or the world?

2. Even though he loves Mary, when the troop of Roman cavalry rides past him Tobias is tempted to follow them. The past still draws him back. Can you put yourself in his place? Do you agree that change is hard?

3. When Mary first sees Elizabeth up above her on the hillside and says the woman's name, Tobias responds, "There is such raw longing in her voice that I no longer want to hold her back." He loves Mary, but he lets her go. Have you ever had to let go of someone you love?

4. In King Herod's courtyard Tobias risks everything by showing his vulnerability. Did this scene mean anything to you personally? Were you surprised by Jeremiah's response? Did you imagine Jeremiah could ever let Tobias go by sending him to Mary?

End with a prayer for those trapped in their past, and thanksgiving for all we've been given.

BONUS ACTION: Close your eyes and try to picture yourself holding in your hands something you truly value. Then open your hands and imagine releasing your hold. Remain in silence with your hands open for as long as you want, then say, with Mary, "Amen. Yes. Amen."

For information on the next volume *Mary's Dog: Bethlehem* go to http://www.MarysDog.com, or follow Mary's Dog on Facebook.

NOTES ON MOLOSSI DOGS

This remarkable breed was originally developed in the ancient eastern Mediterranean world and spread to Rome. In 37 B.C. Roman writer Varro in his *De Re Rustica* gave a detailed description of the Molossi:

"They must be comely in face, of great size, with eyes either darkish or yellowish. Large symmetrical nostrils, lips black with the upper lip neither raised too high or drooping too low. Stubby jaws with large teeth covered by lips, large head and drooping ears. Thick shoulders and neck with thighs long and straight with large wide paws that spread when he walks. A deep bark and wide gape. The backbone neither projecting or swayed, thick coated and of leonine (lion like) appearance."

Virgil, who lived during the time covered by this novel, wrote in his *Georgics* about the Molossi (plural of Molossus), describing their use by both the Greeks and Romans as hunting, guard, and herding dogs. Virgil said, "With them on guard, you never need to fear a midnight thief for your goods, or an attack by wolves, or Iberian invaders at your back."

The Ancient Roman poet Grattius, in his work *The Chase*, wrote: "...when serious work has come, when bravery must be shown, and the impetuous War-god calls in the utmost hazard, then you could not but admire the renowned Molossians..."

In *Epodes,* Horace call the Molossi "the shepherds' dangerous friends."

In *The History of Animals,* Greek philosopher and naturalist Aristotle writes about their courage and physical strength.

For information about one modern-day breed descended from the Molossi, go to http://www.sharakennel.net . Many thanks to Shara Kennel's Zoran Milovukovic for information as well as the photographs used as models for the book's artwork. He writes:

"Shara Kennel has been in existence here in the US since 1990 and was the first to officially show Sharplaninatz dogs at the first ARBA show in Washington DC. However our involvement with this majestic breed dates back to Yugoslavia. Our goal was and still is to produce the dogs that fully live up to the reputation of these legendary guardians from Mount Shara. With this insight, we chose our dogs so we can do all we can to maintain the very essence of the breed."

Also see *Modern Molosser Magazine* at http://www.ModernMolosser.com

FOR FURTHER READING and REFLECTION

- ***In Quest of the Jewish Mary: The Mother of Jesus in History, Theology, and Spirituality,*** Mary C. Athans
- ***Prayers from the Ark and The Creatures Choir,*** Carmen Bernos De Gasztold, Rumer (Translator),
- ***I and Thou,*** Martin Buber
- ***The Miracle of Dialogue,*** Reuel L. Howe
- ***With Open Hands,*** Henri Nouwen
- ***Behold the Beauty of the Lord,*** Henri Nouwen
- ***Immortal Diamond,*** Richard Rohr, O.F.M.
- ***Falling Upward,*** Richard Rohr, O.F.M.

SCRIPTURE NOTES

Gospel of Luke 1: 5-56

Birth Announcement of Jesus the Messiah

26 In the sixth month of Elizabeth's pregnancy, the angel
Gabriel was sent by God to a town of Galilee called
Nazareth, 27 to a virgin engaged to a man whose name was
Joseph, a descendant of David, and the virgin's name was
Mary. 28 The angel came to her and said, "Greetings, favored
one, the Lord is with you!" 29 But she was greatly troubled by
his words and began to wonder about the meaning of this
greeting. 30 So the angel said to her, "Do not be afraid, Mary,
for you have found favor with God! 31 Listen: You will
become pregnant and give birth to a son, and you will name
him Jesus. 32 He will be great, and will be called the Son of the
Most High, and the Lord God will give him the throne of his
father David. 33 He will reign over the house of Jacob forever,
and his kingdom will never end." 34 Mary said to the angel,
"How will this be, since I have not had sexual relations with a
man?" 35 The angel replied, "The Holy Spirit will come upon
you, and the power of the Most High will overshadow you.
Therefore the child to be born will be holy; he will be called
the Son of God.

36 "And look, your relative Elizabeth has also become
pregnant with a son in her old age—although she was called
barren, she is now in her sixth month! 37 For nothing will be
impossible with God." 38 So Mary said, "Yes, I am a servant of
the Lord; let this happen to me according to your word."
Then the angel departed from her.

Mary and Elizabeth

39 In those days Mary got up and went hurriedly into the hill
country, to a town of Judah, 40 and entered Zechariah's house
and greeted Elizabeth. 41 When Elizabeth heard Mary's
greeting, the baby leaped in her womb, and Elizabeth was
filled with the Holy Spirit. 42 She exclaimed with a loud voice,
"Blessed are you among women, and blessed is the child in
your womb! 43 And who am I that the mother of my Lord
should come and visit me? 44 For the instant the sound of your
greeting reached my ears, the baby in my womb leaped for
joy. 45 And blessed is she who believed that what was spoken
to her by the Lord would be fulfilled."

Mary's Hymn of Praise

46 And Mary said,

"My soul exalts the Lord,
47 and my spirit has begun to rejoice in God my Savior,
48 because he has looked upon the humble state of his servant.

For from now on all generations will call me blessed,
49 because he who is mighty has done great things for me, and
holy is his name;
50 from generation to generation he is merciful to those who
fear him.
51 He has demonstrated power with his arm; he has scattered
those whose pride wells up from the sheer arrogance of their
hearts.
52 He has brought down the mighty from their thrones, and
has lifted up those of lowly position;
53 he has filled the hungry with good things, and has sent the
rich away empty.
54 He has helped his servant Israel, remembering his mercy,
55 as he promised to our ancestors, to Abraham and to his
descendants forever."

56 So Mary stayed with Elizabeth about three months and then
returned to her home.

ENDNOTES and POEM

---

[i] **Job 12**, New Revised Standard Version (NRSV©)

[ii] Job 12, New Revised Standard Version (NRSV©)

[iii] Psalm 89, New International Version (NIV©)

[iv] Daniel, New Revised Standard Version (NRSV©)

[v] Psalm 23, New International Version (NIV©)

[vi] Psalm 23, New International Version (NIV©)

[vii] Proverbs, New Revised Standard Version (NRSV©)

[viii] Psalm 148, New American Bible, revised edition© 2010, 1991, 1986, 1970 Confraternity of Christian Doctrine, Washington, D.C. and are used by permission of the copyright owner. All Rights Reserved

[ix] Psalm 131, New English Translation (NEY©)

[x] Psalm 50, New Revised Standard Version (NRSV©)

[xi] Psalm 91, New Revised Standard Version (NRSV©)

Annunciation (a poem for meditation)

Under watchful stars
the untraveled road awaits.
There is no map,
only the whisper of a sound:
an angel's voice
or a dream
or the wind through olive trees.
But she does not hesitate.
In haste, we are told,
In haste
Mary, full of grace, sets out.

-Glenn Lamb McCoy

CPSIA information can be obtained
at www.ICGtesting.com
Printed in the USA
FFOW03n0040091017
40852FF